BLOODY FOOTPRINTS

IN

THE SAND

DECLAN BURNETT

SEVERED PRESS
HOBART TASMANIA

BLOODY FOOTPRINTS IN THE SAND

Copyright © 2021 Declan Burnett

WWW.SEVEREDPRESS.COM

ISBN: 978-1-922551-08-5

43,000 BCE

The snows had melted and the world began to blossom sprouts of greenery. Life forms began to spread, rushing from their thawing hidey-holes to find new, dryer hidey-holes. Many things moved in terror of other life forms: big cats, big lizards, strange beasts with furry backs and huge tusks, and then alphas of their own species. Men and women departed the caves looking for easier food, running in the dead of night, heading south.

Pointless; they'd been watched. From the bushy world around the cave dwelling humans, curious Neanderthals watched their evolutionary betters as they had for many years. They looked so very similar, but they did things that came like magic. They sheltered and fed themselves with a foresight beyond the comprehension of the lesser minds. They kept hidden from predators. They'd many secrets of the universe.

For weeks, the men and women continued south in terror of the large animals stalking them, seeming to understand things that not only kept them safer, but kept the Neanderthals that followed safer by the simple act of mimicry. The sun had come and gone ninety-two times before the men and women settled on a beach with caves, a rock wall, and high but climbable trees.

The lesser-minded followers remained close but avoided contact.

Until the snows came again.

All had a vague memory of the world being cold and food being scarce. Instinct had them gathering where possible and feeding fires offered by the suddenly rare electric skies. The sun no longer seemed to rise as it had, instead it hid behind grey, grey skies. Now, the world lived beneath a sooty day and in the black at night. The men and women rationed and many of the Neanderthals died.

Roots and nuts and the gamey flesh of dead and frozen beasts sustained the men and women a while, but an understanding came upon them and they moved on from the beach. The dry world had extended itself within the frosty atmosphere. They stepped as a tight pack onto the former ocean, for it was smooth and easy to walk upon. Much easier than through the snows on land. The wind bit into them as they moved along the coast and they buried themselves beneath furs. The Neanderthals simply huddled, no longer really hiding themselves at all.

A great storm forced the humans to hunker as the world around them cracked and whistled. The lesser-minded cousins were down to a threesome and, in desperation, crawled into the camp of the men and women. They were accepted, in a way. One of the two males of the Neanderthal trio was weak and became supper for the rest, and the intelligent men and women used their minds. Here they fathomed the herding of livestock to keep meat always within reach. For the female Neanderthal was pregnant and would soon push free a child.

They walked, the men, women, and Neanderthals. The females all gave birth at varying times, and many infants passed very quickly. The flesh of these infants was consumed and gave energy to the group, sustaining life. The surviving Neanderthal children were allowed to live for many months before they were stolen and fed upon.

Nineteen years of walking through the frozen world, the men and women sought berries and tubers and nuts, though ate mostly flesh. The Neanderthals lived in not only terror, but in pain and anger. Understanding and fearing death was enough to keep them in line, keep them from trying for an escape. For where would they go? Sometimes many months would pass before land masses rose from the hardened white world.

For a stretch, the female Neanderthal stopped producing and the men and women had to do hard thinking: to feast or to wait? Waiting paid and the female gave birth to a healthy female child. After three years of mothering, the men and women killed the lesser female and began raising the child themselves. The male was old but his body functioned in both defense against predators and for the needs of procreation—they did not understand that all the barbaric sexual acts taken against the new female Neanderthal stood a chance at making new life, though did understand pairing—and after nine years without a meal of Neanderthal meat, the new female began to show at the belly.

They walked, rarely seeing the sun, but sensing it now and then, until one day it came down upon them like an avalanche and they cowered beneath the brightness as they basked in the warmth. The world around them grew wet. Two days of extreme sunlight had the world cracking and the distant ocean moving again. Four days and the sheet of ice they'd been living upon broke from the shore and they began to drift.

Many young men and women tried to walk upon the ocean as they always had and drowned in thrashing terror. It had been so long since the oceans were free that some had never seen them so had no idea that water could seem bottomless. For once, the old Neanderthal male knew better than most of the men and women of his human overlords. They drifted, still southbound—they'd crossed what would eventually be called the South Atlantic from South Africa, over Antarctica and were now wafting upon the South Pacific. Their platform shrank smaller, and they began rushing upon the surf, covering hundreds of miles in just days beneath the pounding storms that seemed to rise from beneath and pound from above simultaneously.

When they drew close to a shore, the Neanderthal male and his daughter/mate and her son leapt into the water. The child clung to his mother and the mother clung to her father, for he remembered water and swimming. For once, the men and women mimicked the lesser minded male, but they panicked upon striking the water and the Neanderthal stopped swimming once far enough in to walk and watched with rising glee as they perished in terror and pain. Thrashing and wailing.

It was only when on solid shore that the glee disappeared, and was replaced by terror at the incredible roar of a beast.

1

May 3rd, 2002, Terry Williams nodded along to the Nelly track blasting over the in-house system at The Hungry Fisherman bar and grill—the closest thing the town of Prince Rudolf had to a nightclub. On his lap was a young woman named Olivia Robinson. She wore shorts small enough to reveal an inch or so of ass cheek meat and a translucent top that gave anyone close enough a good view of her little pink nipples. Terry was her senior by only four years, so there was nothing problematic there.

But there were problems with this picture.

"If you follow me to the bathroom, I might *go down, down, baby*," Olivia said, hissing it along with Nelly's voice as he sang the hook to *Country Grammar*.

Terry nibbled her ear. Every hot chick between seventeen and twenty-one seemed to want to jump him lately, say over the last three years, and he'd let them. Had been letting them plenty, even chasing them down now and then with a message on ICQ or MSN. The odd one he even telephoned—when they didn't still live with their parents.

Oliva popped up from his lap and danced her way toward the bathrooms at the far side of the dining room that turned into a dance floor every Friday and Saturday night. Terry watched the sway and shake of her butt in those tiny Daisy Dukes and grinned with animal pleasure.

"All right," he said and got up himself.

He cut after her through the throngs of sweaty young men and women, unseeing of any of them beyond shapes. He looked over his shoulder, just in case, and pushed into the women's bathroom. It smelled like cheap perfume, vomit, and farts. The room appeared empty but for a pair of feet behind the one stall door left partially ajar. Terry pushed the door open with his right hand and began unwinding his belt from the loops of his jeans after popping open the big Canada flag buckle.

His pants remained closed and his feet stopped moving. Olivia was there, but behind her standing on the toilet seat was Anna Brandt, his girlfriend who was supposed to be off at university getting her Master's Degree in English for another four days.

Oliva spat on Terry's cheek. "That's for saying you two broke up." She stormed by and Terry leaned away to let her.

"Well?" Anna said.

"Hey, babe," Terry said, maybe a little hopeful.

"Babe? You prick! Four years I've been having hardly any fun at all when I should've been having hot college boyfriends left, right, and center!" she said, stepping closer.

Terry's expression soured. "Yeah, right. I know you were out there whoring it up, that's why I decided tonight was going to be the night I cheated," he said, words a little slurry.

"Tracy Henderson, Ronnie Baker, Susan Becker and Susan Hampton, Denise Robson, Sherry Monk, Christine Matheson, Chelsea Wade and Chelsea Wray. Did I miss anyone?" Anna was tight up close, chests almost pressing.

Terry leaned in to kiss her.

"Fuck off!" she shouted and shoved him.

He tripped, falling hard against the soap-sticky bathroom floor tiles. He blinked up at Anna and Gretchen Bryg. "Where'd you come from?" he said.

"I was standing behind the door, you numbskull," Gretchen said, and kicked him in the ribs.

He squirmed.

Anna jumped with her knees pinning him. "You're nothing. A total nobody. You'll be in this stupid town for the rest of your stupid life," she said and tried to swipe a fingernail down his cheek, but he caught her hand and twisted. "Ow! Let go!"

Gretchen reeled back and punted Terry in the jaw. The crunch was magnificent and his face was no longer uniform. He let go of Anna's hand and lay in a daze. Blood poured from his dislocated jaw, down onto the dirty bathroom floor.

"Yo," Gretchen said, wide-eyed, as if she hadn't been the one to kick him in the jaw.

Anna popped to her feet and grabbed Gretchen by the hand. "Come on, boat's leaving in less than eight hours."

They left the bathroom and then The Hungry Fisherman. They drove Anna's car to her parents' house. From the trunk, they gathered the luggage they'd need for more than two months away and stowed it in the garage. The plan was to share Anna's childhood bed—queen size for the princess of the Brandt family—for the next six hours, just as they had on childhood sleepovers and the occasional drunken high school night.

"Think I broke his jaw?" Gretchen said as she looked out the bedroom window, down the street, and to the lighted Fairview Container Terminal, where the ship Anna's father captained was docked and loaded and ready to set off for the Port of Ningbo in Zhoushan,

China.

"Hope so, but probably just dislocated," Anna said. There were tears in her voice.

Nobody had told her about her boyfriend until that morning and she hadn't believed it until she watched Oliva Robinson come into the bathroom and Terry follow not far behind—Terry had suggested to Olivia that in the very near future he'd be looking to be a one girl kind of guy, so she had been totally game to ruin him.

2

Maurice Brandt was a serious man with a red face and even redder nose. He followed his hard-packed belly into every room but had no trouble squeezing into any of the tight spaces of his ship, anywhere that he'd need to go anyway. He stepped into the kitchen, the coffee percolating, and paused to watch it drip, drip, drip.

"Morning, Captain," Aaron Gunn said. He was the first mate on the ship and was fairly new to the role, was taking it more seriously than he perhaps ought to, given how lax things were on the Chances Taken.

"Hey there, Aaron," Maurice said, not so interested in conversation just yet. He stared down that dark brown fluid, needing it to fill a current vacancy in his being.

"The payload is secured and ready to go. The engineers assured me last night that everything is as good as it can be," Aaron said.

"Really? Both said that?" Maurice said. The damned coffee seemed to be dripping slower than normal. He gave the machine a tap. Something shifted inside and coffee began pouring faster. He smiled.

"Well, Vivian said it's as good as it can be on an old hunk of junk," Aaron said. "Nate just gave me a thumbs up."

The cook, Antoine LeBlanc, stepped into the kitchen with stacked boxes loaded with trays of blueberries. "Fruit is good," he said, French accent thick but intelligible to any English ears, as he continued by to the walk-in cooler, his thick Black arms stark against the white, white fruit boxes and his white, white shirt.

"I hope you don't mind my saying, Captain, but I think she uses cocaine," Aaron said.

The coffee pot was a third of the way full. Maurice grabbed a mug from the rubber-coated counter, blew into it, and then poured a serving of coffee. "*The best part of waking up*," he sang and then took a small, very hot mouthful. "Ahhh." He turned to face his first mate. "I once snorted blow off a stripper's ass, and then her titties, and then down her snail trail to the sweetest tasting—" He stopped and his eyes got wide.

"What is it?" Aaron said.

"Don't repeat that. Don't repeat anything I've ever said. My daughter and her friend are the monkeys on this trip," Maurice said.

From inside the walk-in, Antoine laughed. "I going to tell her about time in Panama. Remember Panama?" He stepped back into the kitchen, grinning like a maniac.

Maurice grimaced and then frowned. "All I remember about Panama is you and…" He trailed, letting their shared memories of debauchery hang, eye-level, like the ripest apple on the tree.

Antoine pulled a face then and waggled his tongue. "You know, I just now forget what I'm thinking."

"What happened in Panama?" Aaron said.

That specific trip to Panama had occurred in 1983. Maurice was unaware he was soon to be a father and Antoine had just started on the ship. Smoking, snorting, drinking, sucking, and fucking; they'd delved deep enough into sexual escapades with some of the locals to test their sexual preferences. Like broccoli: the only way to know a distaste is to have it in your mouth a while.

"Nothing," Maurice said and took another sip from his coffee.

"When your daughter board?" Antoine said.

"Should be here any minute," Maurice said, eyeing the clock above the industrial-sized stove.

"She help me with food?" Antoine said.

"You know, it would be beneficial to load the night before," Aaron said.

In the official hierarchy, Aaron was high above the cook, but in reality, Antoine was number two to Maurice.

"You so green, I mistake you for string bean and put you in my stir fry," Antoine said.

Maurice laughed and Aaron had no retort.

Aaron had labored on the ship three summers before going off to university and coming back educated enough to take over as second mate when his predecessor retired—years before that, Aaron's own father had been first mate. The first mate at the time of Aaron's return was a big, big man who ate one too many orders of dim sum on a stop in China. Aaron became the interim first mate when the man had to stay behind for open heart surgery, and by the time Maurice got around to replacing the suddenly retired first mate, he decided to let Aaron stay in the spot and hire a new second mate instead. Aaron was a bit of an ass, but in a way that got everything that needed done, done. Like a teacher's pet. Every ship needed one.

3

Vivian Montero had one eye on the clock and one eye on the boxy Zenith TV with woodgrain accents. She was sitting on a thrift shop couch at a second-hand coffee table in her mostly barren living room, which was in the basement of a house owned by an elderly couple who charged her $200 a month, cash.

"Yeti, bigfoot, sasquatch, no matter what he is called, many believe he exists," Robert Stack said from the TV screen. He had a great voice, made all the junk about cryptids almost believable.

The old couple who owned the house had a huge satellite dish, pirated and recoded regularly, which meant Vivian could watch just about anything, anything at all. But here she was, watching and rewatching Robert Stack and his endless mysteries. It was her favorite show, and she didn't really understand why.

"Attempts to document bigfoot have, so far, been sketchy," Robert Stack said.

"That's because it doesn't exist," Vivian said and then sighed after casting a glance away from the TV screen. The clock on her VCR told her it was time, so she clicked off the set and grabbed the handle of the luggage she'd prepared the night before. This was going to be her toughest trip, no matter the weather or what complications might arise.

And damn, trouble had arisen lately, creeping out from beneath a party hangover, or more likely a series of party hangovers. At first, she only did it if someone else brought it. Then she bought enough for single nights out. What happened next seemed to happen in a blink. The blow became a daily issue and she'd burned through her savings—including her registered retirement accounts—and maxed her credit cards. She barely had enough to make the two months' rent for the time she'd be gone. In her bulky purse—almost a duffle bag in size—she carried a good number of things, but the most important was the baggy housing twenty grams of coke.

The plan was to wean herself off the drug. Cold turkey hadn't worked, but lessening the amount seemed to be working, at least while at home. She'd only been bonkers out of her mind once in the last month and being in Prince Rudolf had become so boring it made her skin itch these days. So, once in a month was good, better than normal. She had enough coke, if diligently consumed, to take her two thirds of the way across the ocean. After that, she'd have to deal with the shivers and the sickness, if they came. The plan, if executed properly, should keep her from having too bad a time and perhaps let her reclaim a life she was losing her grip on.

4

Nate Stewart slapped Syl Racicot's ass and said, "Get up! Up!"

Syl peeked over his shoulder and then to the clock. "Shit. Antoine's going to be pissed."

Syl was the food prepper and kitchen cleaner. Nate was the second engineer. They'd started dating almost a year ago, after getting caught in the Chances Taken walk-in by Aaron Gunn. He'd seen it his duty to report the situation to the captain. Maurice laughed and told Antoine about the men fooling around on company time and in company space, and for a couple of trips both men caught a little ribbing—*we've got women on the boat so you don't need to*...and *everybody watch your corn holes, here come the bum pirates*—but once the others got used to it, everything went back to business as usual. The ribbing hadn't offended Nate, he'd worked on a few vessels that took longer treks, had played around with a number of lonely men, mostly guys with wives and kids back home somewhere. Syl was a little more touchy, probably because he got it for being of French descent on top of being gay. In the end, the crew had only been getting used to a change in the assumed preferences, and that took time. Nate and Syl were both out of the closet prior, but not to the crew or family, back then it was only under the light of accepting circumstances. At gay bars for instance.

Out the door and running. They each dragged a big suitcase on wheels down the hill toward the pier. Normally, they'd have given themselves enough time for a nice breakfast and a couple cups of coffee, ones not brewed in the clunky old Moffat where the water in the pipes on the ship gave everything a metallic taste. At least Antoine and Maurice agreed upon a variety of coffee brands and strengths, shifting the redundancy onboard just a hair.

Ahead of them, pulling out from a side street was Tess Lachance and her two huge pieces of luggage. She was the medical purser, aka the nurse, on the Chances Taken and treated every day as another opportunity to ply her makeup skills and fashion sense.

"Run, Forrest, run!" Syl shouted, almost running himself.

"She's going to beat us," Nate said.

"Oh yeah?" Syl said a moment before bursting into a sprint.

Nate began running, too, though not at such a torrid pace.

The sun was up and the sea breeze was cool. Seagulls were plentiful but quiet. The traffic was almost nil. The town itself had yet to rise and really get busy with living. Nate loved these moments, and dearly hoped Syl would quit hinting at moving to a bigger city, taking a position on a boat with longer voyages. Two months on and one month off suited Nate, as did the village feel of Prince Rudolf, despite that it was big enough to facilitate a Walmart and a Lowe's. People drove hundreds of miles to visit those stores because heading east was nothing but mountains, and wildlife, and forest. The remoteness let animals thrive. On any given day they might see ten bald eagles, a grizzly bear, and a moose. And that's not to mention the whales or sealions or endless starfish shining up from beneath the docks.

There was nowhere in the world he'd rather call home. Why would anyone prefer a city to the majesty of the more remote regions of the Pacific Northwest?

5

Jane Brandt drove the van. Her daughter Anna was riding shotgun and Gretchen Bryg was in the first row of passenger seating. Most of the crew lived out of town and as a perk, Maurice offered up his wife's services every morning they were to set sail and every afternoon or evening of their eventual return.

"If either of you come back dating any of these lugs, I'll whip your butts," Jane said. "I swear to God."

Anna snorted. She'd told her mother what had happened with Terry, and her mother simply nodded; she'd expected as much for years, but was respectful enough not to get into her grown daughter's business.

"What about pregnant?" Gretchen said, goading the woman.

Anna snickered.

"Dear Lord, save us," Jane said and pulled up a lane that cut into the forest before opening on a settled trailer. The place looked a little nicer every visit—new paint, new porch, new windows, a flowerbed. "Come on, Tim," she said under her breath.

As if hearing it, Tim Kenidi, stepped out of the trailer with a large brown duffle slung over his shoulder. He was one of the ship's laborers and had been on three voyages with Chances Taken.

The sliding door rolled open loudly on its rail. "Hey," Tim said, looking sleepy, his long black hair tied with a piece of black leather. He went to the back row and immediately leaned his head against a wall and closed his eyes.

"Tim, this is my daughter Anna and her friend Gretchen," Jane said.

"I know," he said without opening his eyes. He was only five years older than the pair and had lived his entire life on the Tsimshoo First Nation, right where some British colonizers plopped down a port and called it Prince Rudolf.

"Well, now there won't be any awkward moments of name forgetting," Jane said and put the van in gear. She turned around in front of the home, wheeling onto the grass to do so. Tim still didn't open his eyes. She drove one minute up the gravel road and pulled into an almost identical lane as Tim's, but to a small A-frame home and a lawn littered with toys, an aboveground pool, and a swing set that looked just about rusty enough to disintegrate in a stiff wind. Three dogs lifted their heads from their paws, panting, but didn't move otherwise until the side door of the house opened and a young man hurried out.

Anna and Jane both smiled when the dogs attacked Darvin Lightning with kisses and he dropped like he was shot to roll around with them.

"I gotta go earn the bucks for the dog chow!" Darvin said, laughing.

His wife and kids had come out behind him. His wife was hugely pregnant. The three kids, all in single digits, each latched onto a dog and Darvin got to his feet.

"Bye, love you!" he said and jogged to the van with his luggage.

The door opened and Jane said, "Morning, Darvin."

"Hey. How goes it?" he said, heading on back to sit

with Tim. Darvin had been with the company a few years, was the one who convinced Maurice to hire a couple of his friends to be the other laborers, adding when Maurice seemed unsure: *you can trust us, we're Indians.*

"Pretty good. You know my daughter, Anna. Her friend Gretchen?" Jane said.

"Hey, yeah. I know Gretchen's dad some," he said.

Tim remained leaning, trying to catch a few more seconds of shut eye.

"Hi," Gretchen said.

"Oh, hey, don't mention anything about Carole to Davi, she had to move out," Darvin said.

Davi was the third laborer and the only one Darvin had reservations about when he'd spoken to Maurice— of course he hardly showed it.

"Oh no," Jane said, leaning some and looking in the mirror, hoping for more scoop.

Darvin wasn't dishing and only nodded, pulling a frown across his trim face.

On the far side of what remained officially Nation land, Jane pulled up to a small apartment building that shared a parking lot with a convenience store that sold everything from clothes to pizza by the slice to fishing licenses to postage stamps and Keno cards. Davi was on the crumbling cement steps, waiting, and rose once he saw the van. He slung an old hemp backpack over his shoulder and got in.

Jane made the obligatory chatter, but Davi wasn't much interested. He sat next to Gretchen and watched out the window, his long black hair cascading over his shoulders.

They got two blocks from the terminal and spotted Michael Morse, the watch leader, dragging a canvas Samsonite bag on wheels, big enough to hide the body of a full-grown man inside. Jane pulled over.

"Want a ride?' she said.

"Nah, it's a hell of a nice morning for a walk," Michael said.

Jane nodded and carried on.

42,974 BCE

The two-hundred-pound bear cub was old enough to play on his own and left his mother's side to smell his way around the recently thawing forest. The greens and the rushing water bloomed with new things to see, to touch, to smell, and to chew, and the bear cub was learning that his DNA had code written within his grey matter. There were scripts to follow and games that needed played—practice for dangerous tomorrows to come.

A footlong dragonfly sat on the leaf of a fat bush and the bear cub had the undeniable urge to hunt. He leapt and the dragonfly buzzed away, mostly unbothered. The bear attempted to pop and rebound toward it but stumbled. That fat bush was all leaves and the bear cub crashed through, learning then that the bush partially overhung a cliff. Rolling and bouncing, the bear cub screamed in terror but was pliant enough that the hard bounces hurt it very little. He came to bottom one hundred feet below in a mud patch. The bear cub jerked and kicked, shimmying free…right into a rushing river.

Far overhead, a mama bear wailed for her cub. The cub wailed back but was riding too quickly to grab onto any of the jutting tree limbs or uprising rocks. As if fired, the river shot out over another great drop, this time pointed directly into the ocean.

Splash!

Overwrought, mind scrambled with panic, the bear cub grabbed onto a chunk of lightning struck tree and floated. Distantly, he heard his mama off and on for the next few minutes as the tide pulled him out, sending him adrift. Her voice disappeared and the island began getting smaller.

For eleven days the bear cub floated, starving but too scared to swim away from the log. There were enormous beasts below him and the water was no good to drink. Nothing in his genetic code had prepared him for this.

Land came into view under the full moon on the eleventh night and the bear cub swam with the tide, onto the beach. He slept through the night, and come morning, his instincts came into account again; this time no longer playing. He pounced on a three-foot-wide crab, savagely tearing free its limbs to ingest the wonderful gooey meat within.

In the following days, the bear cub investigated enough of the island to suspect that he had no real predators out there but for time and weather. It was a safely comforting notion, but also a lonely notion.

6

The first day was always the busiest, at least after they'd loaded, and until they reached the destination port. That was if everyone knew their roles. For the first two hours, Anna and Gretchen followed Maurice, they were then passed off to Aaron for twenty-three minutes, and then were summoned—rescued—by Lavell Fraser, the second mate.

He was a dark man of Brazilian heritage, so he assumed. His earliest memories were of the rows of bunkbeds in the orphanage and eating small bowls of steely grey oatmeal. When he was six, an enormous white man picked him out of the line-up of other similar looking children to take him away from the only home he'd ever known. The man lived above a gym and had selected Lavell based on his bone structure with plans on turning him into a steroid infused power lifter and Mr. Universe contestant.

Lavell placed third in the 1994 event and never tried again. He took the $50,000 prize and his father on a trip north, all the way to Alaska—Lavell would be scheduled for paid appearances, though he'd hadn't known that, thought he was doing something nice for his father with the trip. While flexing atop a strip club stage for excited women and amused men, his father and manager—a big, big man who'd finished twelfth in the Mr. Universe Masters section (55+)—was leaned over the bar, chatting up a large woman in a red flannel jacket when he suddenly had a massive heart attack. DOA at the hospital.

There ended the steroids and the competing, though Lavell remained massive by everyday male standards, which was light work by comparison. He relocated to Canada after studying before taking a few different job titles, working on container ships. He took the second mate position on Chances Taken and kept it because it was the first place he'd worked where he wasn't expected to be both a mate and a laborer—though in a pinch he was willing to work his ass off. His deferring menial labor was more of a pride thing.

"Why don't you pretty young things straighten things up here in the grand theatre?" he said, putting sarcastic flair to the word *theeatrah*.

"What?" Gretchen said, laughing.

The room he'd walked them to had two ratty couches and mismatched ratty chairs. At the back of the room was a collection of about 400 VHS movies and 100 paperbacks, with plenty of shelf space for more of each. At the front of the room was a TV. Behind it, the steel wall was painted matte white while everything else was that color of grey that seemed to repel rust.

"See those boxes?" Lavell pointed to the floor where three big brown cartons sat, flaps folded in to reseal the contents.

"Yeah," Anna said.

Gretchen nodded, staring at the bumpy little squiggles of veins protruding from Lavell's outstretched arm.

"Put the contents on the shelf, alphabetically. Then, look busy until supper. I'm sure Maurice has plans for you, but at this minute, we're all doing something we know to do," Lavell said.

"Right," Anna said.

"Right," Gretchen said.

Lavell winked at Gretchen before he left.

Once he was gone, she fell into a puddle with a sigh. "The things I'd let him do to me," she said from the floor.

"He's too big for me," Anna said.

Gretchen spied her friend with one eye. "Good. I don't stand a chance against you," she said.

This had been true, always. Gretchen was a bigger body type, was tall, had wide hips and broad shoulders. Her face was plain at the best of times. Anna was trim but curvy, her lips were pouty and her features perfectly symmetrical. The Greeks would've made statues of her. Everyone wanted her, but she'd only ever wanted Terry—that sonofabitch.

Anna bent over the cartons and pulled apart the flaps. Two had movies, both VHS and DVD, and the other had pocket paperbacks. "You know, I hadn't thought much about what we'd do for entertainment," she said.

Her father had left a standing offer for her to come aboard Chances Taken any summer she liked, earn some bucks and have nowhere to spend it, which worked out better than most jobs. The money earned at summer jobs seemed to light up in her pockets, despite any intentions to save for the coming semesters. She had one full year remaining and the new goal was to graduate with a debt total still in five digits. And, unrelatedly, make up for lost time with boys.

She'd told Gretchen about the job when she hadn't planned to take it, and Maurice told her she could have the spot. Anna hadn't known—though in her deep, deep heart she suspected Terry of being a shit—that she'd suddenly need to be out of town for more than two months and asked if there was room for her. Maurice didn't need two gophers, but if one was his daughter, he'd find a way; couldn't fire Gretchen, of course.

Gretchen crawled to the cartons and looked inside. "Ooh, *Never Been Kissed*. I feel this movie too much."

"You've been kissed," Anna said.

"Yeah, but, like, I've settled. Just because I'm not hot stuff doesn't mean I don't want to make out with hot stuff." She paused a few seconds. "I'm totally going to try to get Lavell. Out at sea, hardly any options, I'll be…" She sighed. "As long as you're not in the room and Tess Lachance isn't in the room, I'll be the hottest chick in the room."

"You're hotter than Tess. She just wears a lot of makeup," Anna said and shuffled the book carton to the shelves of paperbacks already there. She hadn't argued Gretchen versus her, because, well, come on. "You ever read her?" She waved a copy of *Dawn* by Octavia Butler.

"No. I pretty much only read what they tell me to at school…and Nicolas Sparks," Gretchen said.

Anna spun as if jerked. "Oh my god. *The Notebook!*"

Gretchen's eyes grew huge. "They totally need to turn that into a movie!"

7

Darvin bounced into the theater—lounge—in his socked feet, pulling a clothed *Risky Business* as he finished with a slide. "What we watching tonight?" he said, all smiles.

Maurice, Lavell, Vivian, and Tess followed closely behind Darvin. Gretchen and Anna looked at one another. They hadn't picked, obvious now that they didn't know they should've.

"Wait a minute," Maurice said and smacked his forehead with his palm. "I forgot to give you your day one primary objective."

Nate, Syl, Michael, and Davi came in then. They weren't enthusiastic, but Nate and Syl both carried 24-count flats of Budweiser cans. Michael had a box of condiments. Davi was dirty enough that it was best he'd come emptyhanded.

"What's going on?" Anna said.

"Tradition!" Darvin said.

"What about supper?" Anna said.

"Tradition," the usual crew said in unison.

Gretchen laughed nervously.

"What is we watching?" Antoine said. He was carrying a big silver tray with a lid and two bags of hotdog buns pinched between the fingers of his right hand.

"I forgot to tell them to pick a movie," Maurice said, his tone mock grave.

Anna turned around on the couch and looked at the wall of movies. Gretchen leaned in and whispered, "Try to imagine something your father will like or he'll make us walk the plank."

"See, she gets it," Maurice said.

"Uh, what about *Cast Away?"* Anna said.

"We have that?" Vivian said. Her nose was slightly redder than her fair skin.

"I picked it up at Blockbuster, from the two-buck bin. There's movies in there that only just came out. It's crazy. Think it's because hardly anyone wants VHS anymore," Lavell said.

"Anybody see it before?" Maurice said.

"I saw it in the theater," Tess said.

Tim staggered in, his eyes half-closed and his arms covered in dirt. "It's a good one," he said and walked straight to where Antoine had set down the dogs and buns. He took three dogs and three buns, and then grabbed two cans of Bud from Syl's flat.

Everyone quietly watched the man. It was almost as if he was sleepwalking.

"Goodnight," Tim said and was gone.

He'd been in the lounge less than a minute and yet had settled things. They'd watch Tom Hanks and eat dogs and drink beer.

Lavell scooched in next to Gretchen, and even before the plane crashed leaned in tight to her ear. "I was listening outside the door when I left. I think you're the hottest chick in the room, doesn't matter who else is in here," he whispered.

Gretchen stopped chewing and sat still, as if afraid to move, mouth full of hotdog.

"Of course, there's no rush." Lavell leaned away, big grin spreading his cheeks out wide.

Gretchen swallowed the dog and leaned to Anna without looking at her. She tried to whisper, sipped some beer and swallowed again. Finally, she said, "Oh my god, he was listening."

"Who?" Aaron said. He'd popped in to grab a dog—he was to be on the bridge because the captain was watching a movie—and slipped into Anna's spot when she got up to use the can.

Gretchen looked at Aaron with massive eyes and then back to the white spot on the wall where the projector ran the movie. Her cheeks and neck flamed hot, hot red.

"I love this movie," Aaron said and then, "Oops," and got up.

Anna returned and was wiping her damp palms on the legs of her jeans. Once she was settled in, Gretchen leaned over and told both tales of the last two minutes, quietly as she could, finding the full humor of her embarrassment okay because Lavell was going to get it and she was going to give it to him…or more likely take it from him. She was all for it either way.

8

Michael Morse, the watch leader, trudged up the steel stairs, each step echoing hollowly down the long corridor, and up through the door to stand next to Lavell on the bridge. Lavell had been watching the dark waters and the shining sea of lit buttons before him for three hours now. The sun was rising somewhere behind them and had turned everything blue.

"First two days are tough," Lavell said. Moving forward, he'd be on a different sleep schedule from most of the crew.

"Not so bad this time, though, eh?" Michael elbowed Lavell playfully. "That girl Maurice's daughter brought along, I saw you whispering. Were those sweet nothings?"

Lavell, eyes puffy from tiredness, grinned, cheeks pale even with a naturally bronzing tan that clung to his flesh all summer like flies to honey. "It's not so often an opportunity like this comes up."

"Oh?" Michael said. He'd taken his opportunities over the years, even with one member of the current crew. Tess, the medical purser, was a woman in need of stimulation while she waited for someone to get hurt or sick.

"She's just my type." Lavell fell back into the

captain's chair. It was a bulky, wine-colored leather office chair on castors. It had steel framing and real wood accents. Maurice had had it refinished twice now since purchasing the vessel and the chair, fifteen years ago.

"Ah," Michael said.

"I need a woman with some size to her. I'm always afraid I'm going to crush a regular woman. Gretchen is big all over, and in all the ways I like. Get her to the gym a bit, and buy her a blowout, and she'd be ready for prom photos next to me," Lavell said.

"Prom. What are you, thirty?" Michael said. He was in his late forties.

"Excuse you, I'm only twenty-seven, until next week. Pretty sure the girls are twenty-one," Lavell said.

Michael began laughing at a thought. "How fast you think Maurice would throw you overboard if it was his daughter who tickled your fancy?"

"Don't even joke. I'm too heavy. I can hardly swim anymore," Lavell said, then shook his head. "Drowning for some pussy would be a sorry way to go, and I can see myself doing it."

"Rather drown in it," Michael said and immediately felt a little queasy about the phrasing. Nobody on Chances Taken was *that* kind of dude, not really, and he wasn't interested in becoming the one if they had to pick one.

"I'd rather just find the right woman," Lavell said.

"I've done that twice now. Tough being out here with them on land," Michael said.

"Maurice figured it out," Lavell said.

"Maurice figured what out?" Syl Racicot, the cook's assistant, said, coming up the stairs with a pot of coffee and three mugs hanging from his left index finger.

"Marriage," Lavell said and spied the coffee greedily. "Love at a distance."

"That he did. Tough being at sea with a partner on

land," Syl said, unintentionally parroting Michael. Before he'd rescued Nate Stewart, the second engineer, from the closet, he'd had more than a handful of failed relationships.

"That's what I said," Michael said.

"Got any creamer?" Lavell said.

Syl had set the coffee pot and mugs on a clear spot of desk space and reached into the pocket of his loose cotton pants that featured a tight, black and white checkerboard pattern. He set out four creams and six sugar packets—he knew what everyone onboard took, everyone but for the new girls. Give it a few days and he'd know that, too.

"True love that works at a distance, that's some rare stuff," Michael said. He sipped from his mug and added, "Ahh, got to love that tinny pipe water."

"I don't even taste it," Lavell said. "Not anymore…can't be that rare, true love at a distance."

"Rare as a sasquatch," Syl said and lifted the half-empty coffee pot. "Top up? I've got to start breakfast prep."

42,973 BCE

The Neanderthal male lay in a bloody heap as the mother and her son cowered at the shore of the island that should've been their salvation. He moaned, his breath hitching and his hands exploring the various causes of his impending demise, until he lay flat and died.

The immense bear cub turned even bigger bear had spent a year alone on the island, following its wits and what it discovered within its DNA. Its first thought was to crush all these interlopers, but beneath the fresh, hot, hot blood of the male, it smelled something on the female. A fishy scent that clicked a primordial need that had only been assuaged by him rubbing himself against certain rocks and smooth, oily trees.

The bear leaned its blood-dripping snout into the fur-clad lap of the mother and then to the son. The son carried a strange absence of scent and the bear returned to the hot-smelling place on the mother.

The Neanderthal mother shook in terror but had experienced this before and acted accordingly—it had saved her from beatings by the human men on the floating ice shelf. She moved slowly, dropping to her hands and knees and stuck her backside in the air.

The bear sniffed and followed the road map laid out

by its genetics. It pressed weight upon her back, flattening her into the sand.

The mother screamed as the bear clawed her back while penetrating her but did not fight the act. In the years to come, the flesh of her back would grow tough with scar tissue and her body expectant with pleasures. The boy Neanderthal survived seven years on the island with the female and the bear before succumbing to the fresh bout of horrid cold that froze the world and stole most of their food.

Survival mode had the female doing things she'd seen the men and women do before they drowned in the thawed ocean. The cave bear worked from the limited memories it harbored and with codes of its DNA. They became a team.

The bear killed fish and birds, and they fed. The female made clothes and watched the skies for electricity. Together they chased fire when it came to the island. They hunkered and starved and mated and slept. After nine years, something changed with the bear's seed and something changed within the female's womb and with her eggs. Her belly grew huge with pregnancy.

For the following twenty years, the female birthed a furry child every ten months, almost half of them survived. The bear died and the female lived on until giving birth in her thirtieth year became the act that finally killed her. The surviving offspring did as they always had with their dead: they feasted upon the flesh. But this time they kept the bones. That mother had been so very different from them, she had been wiser than they were and craftier with tools.

The offspring of the bear and the Neanderthal mated. And mated. And mated.

While the deep freeze remained over the island and the world beyond, for the following two thousand years, many of the beasts departed, trailing the marks left by great mammoths trudging upon the ice. Many more of the beasts simply walked, chasing the possibilities of the unknown.

By the time the two-thousand-year freeze ceased, only six beasts remained on the island. They'd learned to remember. They gathered food and burned the excess in their dens. They minded fires to keep them ablaze until finding fire rained down from electric skies regularly.

The thaw had lasted six hundred years and the beasts thrived, forgetting their food caches and ignoring the fires. When the next great frost hit, it stung and many beasts died, but not all.

9

Anna looked at her hands. The blisters were weeping and angry, even around the various bandages Tess had affixed to the sore spots. Anna then looked at the mop handle that had seemingly become another appendage of her body these last eight days. She'd cleaned more than she had her entire life and repeated it ten times over. Especially since Gretchen was shirking her duties to sneak off to Lavell's cabin.

Anna begrudged her only momentarily. Gretchen had never, ever, ever been someone's choice cut in the butcher shop window, whereas Anna could've been prominent on any dinner plate…had she not wasted so much time with that asshole, Terry. At least she'd quit crying about it for now and she had to think that soon she'd heal to the point of not thinking about him at all. To spur it along, she'd even considered having a boat fling.

"You are gorgeous, but I ain't losing my job," Tim said, then yawned as he turned away from her one night after supper in the hull.

Embarrassed, Anna said, "Sorry. I'm out of practice with playful flirting…I didn't…I mean…"

Tim gave a brief consideration over his shoulder, but only nodded at her and refocused on the mystery leakage spilling from one of the containers; smelled like apple juice, but that didn't make much sense given what was on the manifest.

Anna decided she'd give her hands a break and wheeled the mop and bucket to the closest utility closet. She wondered if her father always demanded the boat shine or if this was a rarity. Busy work. She hit the light switch and stepped inside the closet. She sat on stacked boxes of rough brown paper towel rolls. The chemical scents settled in her chest, reminding her strangely of a specific bar soap, the kind…Terry's absence crashed into her. She was wrong, the tears hadn't passed.

Oh, Christ, she'd wasted so much time on him. She took a deep breath and tried to steady her chin. It didn't work; she bawled like a baby, her face pressed into the shoulder of her t-shirt. She didn't even know how to flirt with guys anymore, and Terry had been flirting—and so much more—the whole time they'd been together, apparently. She'd gotten a dozen texts since she'd dumped him—on the bridge, she had full bars, though was warned to keep the phone off, was likely on the Chinese government network, or the Russian government network…or just AT&T and she'd owe a bundle once she got the bill. Word got around in a place like Prince Rudolf. It almost seemed as if these people were happy to finally tell her all the nasty shit they'd seen Terry doing behind her back, and not out of a sense of loyalty or sympathy, but to point a finger at perfect Anna Brandt.

Thinking about them shifted things a little and that was all right; better to be mad than sad, better by a longshot.

"Fuck all of them," she mumbled and flicked the light off in the closet, thinking if she could, she'd leave that little piss hole in a snowbank town forever. Let her parents visit her at Christmas, wherever she settled.

She walked, swaying in tune with the ocean

carrying them along. She wiped her face and took five more deep breaths. Better. On top of everything, she'd gotten sick on the second day when she was scrubbing the hidden spaces of the walk-in cooler and then the chest freezer. Something about the food smells mixing with the rhythm of the water really had her guts roiling. She felt like a failure for it, like she'd shed an important part of her genetics, but her father had come to see her shortly after and said, "One time the deep freeze went out when we were on a five-day stopover and Antoine had to clean out pounds of rotten meat when we came back aboard. He was taking it like a trooper, but I barfed as soon as I stepped over the kitchen threshold."

She figured his point was right: not the ocean but the smell—though in that deep spot where sour-tasting truths lived, she knew it was a bit of both. She headed up to the deck for some air and to put her hands on the cool steel of the railing. She'd liked it up there, since getting out of seagull poop-range, though clean or messy, the sea-scented air was wonderful and seemed to clear everything negative from her mind.

She stood at the side, watching the emptiness fly by. It was so peaceful and calming. She sighed as she squeezed the cool handrail. Not fifty feet from the ship, a humpback pod breached and the largest of the bunch flopped backward, showing off. The others began to mimic.

"Never get sick of that," Darvin said.

The ocean was so loud and the engines of the Chances Taken were even louder, it was difficult *not* to sneak up on people.

"I know, right?" Anna said. "Did Dad see these?"

"Yep. Just announced 'em inside and I was already over here," Darvin said.

Antoine hurried through a heavy door in his cook's whites. "Ooh, that's nice."

The humpbacks had fallen behind—weren't trying to keep up—but it was simple enough to see them in all that empty water.

"Got to feel sorry for people who never get to see that in the wild," Darvin said. "It's not the same on video."

"Not close at all," Antoine said. "Not even aquarium near as good."

The peace around them was heavy and lulling, like the perfect blanket against the fresh, soft, soft skin of a baby. Until the crashing, grinding sounds rang out and the arm horn blared its siren call. The whales were instantly   forgotten.

10

Rationing her stash was not going as planned for Vivian. Being on the water, with the crew, them drinking and laughing, should've made it easier, but it had the opposite impact. She'd already snorted half the coke she'd brought, and they were only eight days in. This stressed her. The added stress intensified her ache for chemical enhancement.

It also intensified the number of times she'd found herself in rooms unaware of how she'd gotten there. The most troubling had been the engine room. She'd come to after she'd envisioned, daydreamed even, almost felt herself working a sabotage mission against the vessel's heart, as if that might take her home and back within reach of her dealer. In fact, she'd found herself in the engine room not half an hour ago, with greasy hands and a blank spot in her memory. There was a hammer on the floor before her. The engines were raging, clanking angrily.

"Fuck it," she said once back to her room. That all had to be in her imagination, no way she'd ever do something so pointlessly reckless.

She tapped a rail with her dirty hands from the clear baggy onto the shaving mirror she kept in her dresser— she planned to say, if anyone ever asked, that it had been in a drawer when she put her stuff in, wasn't hers at all, didn't have a clue as to how it got there. She pushed the small white mound into a line with her laminated Prince Rudolf library card. She rolled a clean chunk of paper into a tube and put it into her open nostril like a straw. Why people treated both nostrils when only one was ever open, she never understood.

She snorted the powder away, jerking her head back as the wonderous energy coursed through her. She huffed two quick breaths and then licked the face of the mirror clean. The residue tingled on her tongue. She then opened the paper and ran her tongue along the cocaine's route, getting every molecule of happiness.

As she was swiping her tongue for a second coke check, the warning alarm sounded after a great bang and thump shook the steel walls of the vessel. She looked around her tiny cabin, thinking, *what have I done?* and having very little of a clue of what exactly she had done.

She stashed the baggy and the mirror. She crumpled the paper and dropped it on the floor beneath the hammock she used only on especially rocky nights. Through the cabin door into the hallway, she ran. Ahead of her was Nate. He wore only his boxer shorts and an off-white undershirt—his shift was overnight, but that siren demanded his attention. When it came to breakdowns, he was second only to the chief engineer, Vivian Montero, cokehead extraordinaire.

She looked at her hands, suddenly painfully aware that they were still greasy from whatever she'd done. Dammit. She had to get in there and get to fiddling with dirty things before anyone noticed. She let the chemical influx work her legs into overdrive. She reached the engine room only a step behind Nate. Smoke poured free from the doorway and a small fire licked out against the steel walls and ceiling. A bad situation wasn't getting worse; no cover like smoke cover.

She chased in and grabbed the second fire extinguisher from the wall and began spraying. The fire died quickly, and she dropped the extinguisher, let it clank off the floor before she fell to her knees to reach around blindly within one of the engines, as if she might suddenly find something.

"What are you doing?" Nate said, almost yelled it, his voice echoing against the now eerie quiet of the engine room.

"Fuck, I don't know. Something fucked up, maybe a bolt dropped into a gear or something," she said, though she had no doubt the trouble had to do with the heavy ballpeen hammer on the floor and a few bent piston arms within the block. The kind of damage that would break even thick steel as pistons slammed, sending chunks of shrapnel that would rattle around the engine blocks, possibly busting holes, but at minimum cracking them.

Why she thought these things had happened, she didn't dare explore, not aloud anyway.

"See anything?" Nate said.

"Only trouble," Vivian said, wondering if she'd said that too quickly, or perhaps she'd said it oddly, suspiciously even. "What. A. Mess." This she said slowly, really pausing and accentuating.

11

The Chances Taken drifted, still heading westbound, for fifteen minutes before the last of the push wore off over the calm, calm ocean. The humpbacks had followed at a distance and had now caught up to them, splashing a show that nobody witnessed. The entire crew, both day and night portions, were either within the engine room or the hall outside the engine room.

"Well, damn," Maurice said and stood from where he'd been crouched to look at the troubled set of engines. The third engine had a cracked block but was possibly salvageable. There was an auxiliary engine that would putt them along, which would need to be installed after the other engines were removed. "Damn," he said again as he stepped to the doorway where Tess and Antoine stood on either side.

"Well?" Darvin said from a foot into the narrow hallway.

"I guess you, Tim, and Davi should hang around here while Vivian and Nate get busy cleaning up this mess," Maurice said.

"Too far out for a tug?" Darvin said.

"We're almost halfway, whole lot of nothing out there. Cost three or four times what I'll lose already to pull us in," Maurice said.

"There's an island," Michael said. He'd been up top until the boat lost most of its momentum.

"Oh?" Maurice said.

All others were silent, as if someone had died. The scent of burnt oil was heavy amongst the greasy metal scents that were typical of the vessel, and the air in the hallway harbored lingering smoke that never got to rise above eight feet.

"You're going to want to have a look. There're signs of people. Not now, but maybe from the forties or fifties, maybe older," Michael said. "I couldn't tell much through the binoculars, but there's definitely a dock."

Maurice gave an absent nod. "All right, let's get busy. If you're not helping with the engines, stay out of the way."

"What do you mean by people? More than just a dock?" Aaron said.

"Like signs, with words. Japanese, I think. And a gate," Michael said.

"Weird," Anna said absently.

A new excitement began to build after the great emotional fall of suspecting they'd add a couple weeks to the trip, at minimum. At least there might be something to see while they were stuck out there.

"Best go call our location in, if you haven't," Maurice said.

Aaron, who'd been walking just behind Maurice, took a left and raced away from the group, perpetual busy beaver. His footfalls echoed hollowly away like a passing rain shower, the volume warbling up and down as the sound waves impacted upon the steel walls, ceiling, and floor.

Everyone else continued on toward the bow and the grated steel staircase that led upward to the deck. With every step, it seemed, the group's pace increased. Feet thumped and that hollow metallic ring spoke of each step upon the staircase. Something to see was something to see.

The door at the top opened a momentarily blinding cast of white light upon the crew, halting the forward motion for one, two, three seconds. The island was clearly visible with the naked eye, but nothing of what the watch leader had described was apparent.

"Here," Michael said and handed over the binoculars.

Maurice accepted them, belly leaned against the bow's handrailing. A bit to the south of their trajectory was the island. It was small, perhaps the size of a hobby farm that still brought in crops. On the north shore were a series of rusty steel docks. Beyond them was asphalt overrun with flora. Grasses and saplings jutted from the surface like alfalfa at the back of a head. Past that were the gate and the sign. The gate still had some paint left on it. The sign's writing was indeed in huge Japanese characters, though below, it looked something like English.

"Anna, your eyes are better than mine. I think that sign says something in English beneath the Japanese stuff," Maurice said, holding out the binoculars.

Anna stepped forward as the crew watched her in silent fascination. She accepted the binoculars and refocused. Squinting. Hard to tell for sure, but... "Uh, I think it says, 'Land Fun Pacific.'" She rolled the binoculars around the island. The white sandy beach, the thick palm trees, the Ferris wheel. "There's a Ferris wheel!"

"What?" Maurice said.

The crew grumbled, almost in unison.

"Look," Anna said, pressing the binoculars into her father's chest, eyes still on the island.

Maurice looked, scanning, and there, amidst many tall trees, was what appeared to be a Ferris wheel. "Well, I'll be damned."

12

The anchor went down; the jarring rattle of the chain was extreme against the calm of the ocean. Lavell and Antoine drew back the cover from the lifeboat. All but the engineers, the laborers, and the second mate piled into the smallish vessel, which could be cranked down and back up from within the hull. Going down was a touch alarming and more than one member of the crew kept their eyes forward.

The splash was gentle, as was the lapping once they were securely in the ocean. Everyone within reach of a rope connected to the lower basket grabbed and pulled the boat forward. Once clear, Maurice lowered the 12 horsepower Evinrude engine into the water. With a single yank of the recoil cord, they were off, buzzing across the smooth space between boat and island.

They'd gathered things before they left, just in case. They had a cooler full of food and a case of bottled water. They had machetes and bug spray and thick leather gloves. They had two .306 rifles—handled by Syl and Michael. They had a large first-aid kit.

The closer they drew, the more impossible the aspects of this island became. It looked older than from the 1950s. Maybe as old as the 1930s. Everything was rundown, but by time rather than by use. It appeared to have been an abandoned tourist stop, which was crazy. Who could get all the way out here for a vacation? Like putting a 7-Eleven on the moon.

Maurice eased off the throttle and coasted to about twenty feet from the docks. There was something strange and off-putting about the scene. At least from the front. Distantly, it appeared most of the fifty or more acres were covered by foliage. The Ferris wheel was smaller than normal and appeared flimsy once close enough to see it clearly with the naked eye. The cars were pocked by rust holes and looked too thin to hold any kind of weight. Against the thickness of the docks and the gate—heavy duty steel, that was obvious even from a distance—the Ferris wheel seemed like a model, a replica that was for show and not use.

"What's a theme park doing out here?" Tess said. She had the travel first-aid kit in her lap, open, as if she worried that she'd forgotten something vital.

"Guess we'll find out," Maurice said and twisted his wrist to juice the throttle.

They pushed on, a gentle breeze playing their hair back while they passed over the gentle waters to what appeared to be a gentle step back in time.

13

"Figure one going must've bent the other piston rods and chain-reacted," Nate said. He held one of the wonky culprits up for the others to see. He had been sitting but needed to move into a couch as the puddling oil finally leaked enough to travel to the front side of the engines. "There's a few dozen bolts that need to come out, but it's not too bad. Real struggle is hoisting the engines out of the way. Probably be wise to wet vac' everything up."

"You in charge now?" Tim said, smirking.

Nate shook his head as if to say *who knows?* rather than *no.*

The squeak of the rolling engine hoist's wheel crept closer, cheeping like a mouse. Vivian had gone to grab the bulky unit because being around people was messing with her brain. She needed to clear her head and think about what she'd done and why—soon she'd get to how crazy and stupid it was, but for now, she was a little bit high and a lot scared. Scared not just of what might happen to her but also scared of what was going on inside her brain. What kind of ship engineer destroys engines in the middle of the Pacific? What a mess.

"Here she is," Davi said, and the trio of laborers

stepped out of the doorway. They each held a small toolbox, awaiting orders.

Vivian rolled the hoist into the engine room, directly above the first engine. She took a deep breath as she looked at the piston Nate held up to her, like it was proof of her guilt, an accusation of crime.

"Look at that thing. Sheared right off. I'm guessing the rest is inside the block," Nate said.

Vivian couldn't look and wasn't about to touch it, not again. She instead turned to the wall boxes and opened the first that housed a built-in air-compressor. She began unwinding the cord. As she did so, Tim set down and kneeled before the toolbox he'd carted. He withdrew the brushed steel ratchet gun. It was heavy and old, older than him. Vivian held out the hose with the coupler end to him. If anyone recognized the oddity to this role reversal—she was the chief engineer and was acting like a laborer's apprentice—none of them mentioned it.

"One and a quarter for those," Nate said and stood up straight to get a look at the third engine where the piston hadn't broken through. He whistled.

"How bad?" Darvin said.

"Might get lucky. Have to take it apart, clean it, and cement it. You ever take apart an engine?" Nate said, looking up to Darvin and Davi, both still holding toolboxes housing task specific sets.

"Not that big," Darvin said.

"Big makes it easier. It's the same as an old truck," Nate said.

Darvin and Davi both nodded. They'd had trucks and had worked on trucks that didn't belong to them in the past. If it weren't for a disinterest in moving from home and all the school they'd have to do, they might've been mechanics.

The air compressor kicked in and all chatter ceased instantly. It was nearly as loud as all three engines running. Hard to say if it was better or worse that they were on a smaller vessel; on one hand, a bigger vessel had more engines, which meant more back-up power; on the other hand, more engines might've meant more to break, more chances at supreme destruction.

Vivian appreciated the lack of talk, but the noise grated at her, seemed to call to her. God, how good would it be to shut out everything, surf the snowy waves of a mound of coke?

"Probably somebody should grab the shop-vac!" Nate said, looking at the laborers crouching over the engines.

Vivian snapped to. "I'll grab it!" She hurried away again, would take her time coming back. Might even detour to her cabin for a pick-me-up.

14

Antoine tied the lifeboat to one of the rusty dock posts and held them steady while the others climbed out.

"What do you think, go to the beach and have a listen?" Lavell whispered. Gretchen was tight at his side, almost touching him.

Maurice gave a slow nod, though didn't look at the man. All eyes were on the gates and beyond. What in the hell was this place? The sign did indeed state that it was LAND FUN PACIFIC but nothing about that fit.

Birds and the gentle lap of the ocean, they heard nothing else. Maurice motioned to Syl and Michael to lead the way through the gates—they had the weapons after all. A slight breeze rustled the weighty fronds sprouting from the trees, swishing like knives through fabric. The sand was loose beneath their feet until they reached the crumbling asphalt of the once civilized instalment. The sun had bleached it light grey.

It took about five times longer than would be normal for the crew to walk from the dock to the gates. They were curious and cautious, eyeing anything and everything for more oddities. And why did they even need gates? It wasn't as if anyone was going to make the trip without a ticket to get inside. Weird. Did they once even sell tickets to this place?

The gate was mechanical and took force to push it open, popping springs with the effort—once stretched beyond the limit, it swayed loosely on its post. Everywhere they looked, the plant life had overgrown the human elements, but a few carnival game stalls remained obvious by their shapes, and a few squat buildings filled in behind them. There was a teacup ride next to the Ferris wheel. This only added to the mystery while simultaneously emboldening the point to an earlier note.

Now, this close, it was wholly apparent that if anyone ever rode these rides, they were small and still did so at their own peril. They were like props to a film.

"Something not right here," Antoine said. "Something fishy fishy."

"I wouldn't trust that Ferris wheel with my dog," Tess said.

"You have a dog?" Michael said.

"Yeah, my mom watches him…guess he's more like her dog now," Tess said.

"It's almost like it's made of those connector toys from when I was a kid," Maurice said. "Think they shot a movie way the hell out here?"

"Seems highly irregular, don't it?" Michael said.

"Connector toys? The steel ones you bolt together?" Gretchen said and Maurice nodded. "I found a whole bin of those in my grandma's basement when she died. I think my dad sold them to a guy at the Prince George Flea Market."

"Has to be fake, right?" Tess said. "Even if it's not from a movie set, it's not something you'd ride."

"But why then?" Maurice said.

Anna blinked, the cogs of her grey matter kicking the tires of some buried knowledge. And then something she saw about Russians during WWII on the history channel clicked in and became words. "Holy shit, I think I know," she said.

Everyone looked at her. "What is it, hun?" Maurice said.

"Let's check in one of the buildings before I say. I don't want to feel like an ass," Anna said, blushing. If it were only she and her father, she'd say what she thought, but with everyone else there, she didn't want to risk it.

"Which one?" Michael said.

"Start with the closest," Maurice said. "And maybe get some of the bug spray out, we might have to make a run for it if there's bees or wasps or something."

"How would they get here?" Tess said.

"How do things get any place?" Antoine said.

Gretchen, Anna, and Lavell swung around their packs. Gretchen and Lavell brought out green aerosol cans of Deep Woods spray while Anna pulled out the red and yellow aerosol can of Raid. They moved slowly, as if approaching an open door on a tiger cage. The gunners stepped aside and let their captain try the door handle upon arrival.

To the collective surprise, the door clicked open. Dim inside, but the broken windows let in enough light to reveal rows of steel bunkbeds, trunks resting at the foot of each. Broken fronds and twigs had found their way inside, as had ants that had busted up through the cement floor. At least there was nothing Anna's can of Raid couldn't handle. Not that she cared to kill these particular ants. They weren't hurting anyone.

"Who would come here?" Maurice said, thinking aloud.

"Almost like a dorm or an orphanage or something," Michael said.

Maurice tapped an index finger against a door. "Well, is it what you think?"

All turned to Anna. "Maybe. I want to check one of the game booths first…but I'm pretty sure."

"You don't need to play coy," Gretchen said, teasingly.

Anna wrinkled her nose. The group had eased a good deal since docking and learning what little they had so far. Michael and Syl led the way to the closest game booth and its side door. Maurice, giving off an air of comfort, of nonchalance and safety, turned the handle and shoved open the door without ceremony. It was total dark inside where the light from the doorway didn't touch.

"Flashlight? Anyone think to bring one?" Maurice said.

"I bring lighter," Antoine said.

Maurice held out his hand, palm up. "Anyone have paper to burn, or see any paper to burn?"

Antoine withdrew his cigarette pack and lit a Matinee Gold, then handed over the lighter. Gretchen pulled a copy of a Dean Koontz novel from the ship's library and shrugged.

"I started this one but it's not very good. It's all like *I wish women wore dresses and stayed home with the kids* and every woman is supermodel beautiful and home invasions happen, like, hourly... If you don't mind burning it, I grabbed it from the lounge," Gretchen said, rambling, somewhat embarrassed.

Maurice accepted it. "Who is it that reads the Koontz books?" he said.

"Nate does," Syl said. "But he's read that one, I think. I remember him telling me about it seeming like Koontz was terrified of home invasions...though, now that I think about it, I think he said Koontz has several home invasion books. The women are always perfect, too."

Maurice paused to consider it a moment before tearing away the cover and about ten pages from within. "Come up here, Anna," he said and then lit a corner. He stepped into the room, slim behind the game booth, and revealed several dozen domed helmets, utility belts, and forest green rifles. "Holy cow."

"I was right," Anna said. "Okay, so, it happened before this, I think. I think I know. I think so. Anyway, in the Second World War, the Russians painted trees and plywood to look like huge munitions stockpiles. I was thinking…I also saw this other one about American strongholds on Pacific islands, like half the islands are still radioactive now. I think."

"Why?" Gretchen said, scrunching her face.

"Why'd they—?" Anna began but was cut off.

"No. Why you watching that stuff?" Gretchen said.

Anna could only shrug. Mostly, she watched whatever was on.

1945 CE

The prefabricated pieces came off the civilian ship quickly and smoothly. The soldiers, topless while laboring in the heat, and wearing only hemp shorts and leather boots, worked like single-minded ants. They were further east than was safe, but sonar suggested some time and they had to trust in the plan—even if they didn't, orders were orders. It took three days to move all the munitions into the underground caches, including several ground missiles that, if mishandled, housed enough power to destroy the island several times over. Which wasn't an issue, according to the brass. Soldiers, especially grunters like the ones installed on the island, were expendable while assisting the greater good. If the island itself disappeared it caused no real problem either, as no country claimed it. Up until two months prior, it had been unmapped and assumedly unvisited. Fun Land became its official title and Japan claimed it as part of the country—despite being almost three thousand nautical miles from home.

It took only a week to finalize the various elements of the ruse. The brunt of the soldiers left the island, leaving behind seven men to listen to radio transmissions and watch the waters. If the call came, their missiles could destroy any manner of aircraft coming for retribution after their attack on Hawaii. An attack they'd been anticipating for many months already.

The remaining men were on the island for only two days when the first animal strike occurred. Nobody saw it, but a soldier named Kenji Motoe had strayed to the periphery of where they'd touched and civilized thus far, what they were calling the fairgrounds, and unzipped his fly while the others were tamping down asphalt. He'd been pissing and that's all anyone could say for certain.

The corpse was shredded and what remained above the waist were gristly, gnawed upon bones. Several bloody footprints leaving the scene were also added in the report. Massive, ape-like, bear-like, prints. The following day, three men entered the thick bush with rifles in hand but found nothing beyond birds to fire upon and coconuts to collect, unaware they had been monitored and studied by fascinated creatures, ones much smarter than any animal they'd encountered before.

The morning following, four men awoke to find two men missing. They called it in, but many days would have to pass before any help arrived, and a war was on; sending troops to an out-of-the-way cache site was not top priority. The soldiers slept in shifts, but underestimated the hunter or hunters prowling the island. The awake soldiers watched the trees at the rear of the fairground and the beach leading back to the Pacific. For several nights, every twig snap and every gust of wind riled their hackles and they aimed rifles at ghosts.

By the fifth night, two men remained on watch while two men lay on bunks in the barracks. Unlike before, they'd closed the door, despite the roiling heat. Sleep came eventually for this pair with thanks to pilfered drugs from the aid closet at the back of the communications office, hidden by a ring toss game.

Taro Uto and Hiroo Honda stood beneath the huge, rather weak spotlights powered by water wheels installed beneath the docks. They held much more powerful flashlights alongside their rifles.

"What do you think?" Taro said, voice low but not quite a whisper.

"My grandmother would probably say it's a sea demon."

"Crazy talk."

"I think it is an American bear," Hiroo said, before lifting a cigarette to his lips and dragging hard.

"How does a bear get here?" Taro said, lowering his rifle and flashlight to fish into his shirt sleeve for his cigarette pack and lighter.

"Zookeeper from Australia. He goes to America and buys animals, but on way home has trouble and has to stop near this island. Maybe the bear goes crazy and they force it off the ship," Hiroo said. He let the flashlight sweep gently over the lifeless forest. Whatever trouble had come almost seemed behind them now.

"Maybe it's Oni," Taro said through an exhaled cloud of smoke.

"You think there's an ogre here?" Hiroo turned his light on Taro.

Taro was all smiles. "Yeah, and it's right behind you!"

Hiroo didn't believe it but spun and made rifle blast sounds with his mouth. "Get it. All hail Hiroo the hero," he said and turned back.

Taro was swallowing heavily. Behind him, thick teeth encircling his neck, was a furry creature with humanoid hands and a long, domed cranium with beastly mannish face below. Taro dropped his rifle and flashlight. His knees buckled. The thing held him, feasting slowly as blood ran in cascading waves over his shoulders. Hiroo dropped his own flashlight as he raised his rifle to fire. He felt hands on him, felt clawed nails pierce the flesh of his chest. He let out half a scream before those great furry hands latched onto either side of his ribcage and pulled outward, spilling the man like a briefcase with a broken latch.

Hiroo looked down at his guts, the deep, deep red splash upon the sand, thinking he'd get an infection, his organs getting dirty like that. His eyes trailed closer and down his abdomen, and he saw the lightning pace of his beating heart beneath the dim spotlights. It looked like a shiny piece of black volcanic glass. The beast holding him let him fall back and then pounced on his hips. Its face lowered but held eye-contact with Hiroo as it bit away the delicious dangling fruit that was his heart.

A few feet away, three beasts feasted on Taro. Further yet, four more beasts were trying the skills they'd learned from observing the soldiers. The door handle worked with surprising ease and the beasts stalked into the dorm and to the sleeping men. The fight was over before either man knew they'd been in it.

15

Vivian had oil up to her elbows and all down her front, and everywhere else she'd wiped or scratched since they'd begun dismantling the engines. The unladylike-ness of the scene made her think of the second grade. She'd been adamant with her mother that, despite being ill, she wasn't missing the year-end presentation. Rather nervously, her mother fed her four Imodium tablets and four shots of Pepto Bismol, was ready to do another round but apparently the scoots had quit scooting. Still, the girl looked green enough that Vivian's mother was considering stopping at the drug store for a box of Depends—even if Vivian wasn't worried, her mother foresaw students having very, very long memories about one of their classmates shitting herself onstage.

Vivian spotted her mother in the front row after they'd arrived at school just in time for the bell that would send the kids to their final class and to slip Vivian into her costume. With her name coming midway through the alphabet, she watched from the wings as a dozen students from her grade, mostly in half-assed costumes and half-assed understandings of what the job they wanted to do when they grew up entailed, stepped onstage and belted out explanations.

When it was her turn, Vivian clenched her sphincter muscle tight and swished front and center. She had a huge clear plastic bowl over her head. The bowl had been taped onto a carboard box covered in tinfoil that fit over her abdomen. Her arms were bare and below her waist was a pink tutu with white leggings.

"My name is Vivian Montero, and in the future, people will take trips to space for fun, and I will be the first woman to dance in space," she said and then, still clenching, jumped up and fell into the splits. The crowd applauded loud enough that they didn't hear the wet, wet fart. Vivian's mother caught the expression on her daughter's face and broke from her seat.

However, like a resilient social standings veteran and not like a second-grader, Vivian pushed to her feet and bowed and curtsied as she backed into the shadows and cut through the center stage drapes instead of falling off to the wings as was the practiced route. She met her mother in the hallway and together they rushed out to the car.

Vivian stayed interested in space but had succumb to the reality of disposition. Some dreams simply were too difficult to obtain for people. She was still enthusiastic about mechanics and understood how things worked. She studied hard and, while in school at least, kept her nose clean. But she was never the top in her class, and certainly not the top of any high-flying space-specific focuses. She'd left her tutu behind and only got high as space in the mental sense.

"Fuck," she whispered. The reality of what she'd done was hitting her again; pounding her over and over. She'd have to go to rehab; this would have to be her last trip for a long while. She couldn't be trusted.

But what of the blow left in her room…

"I need a break," she said. They'd been at it for hours and what was happening now was mostly up to the laborers.

"Yeah?" Nate said. He'd gone off to put on pants after about twenty minutes of work, laughing at himself as he did so. "Guess you'd be off now, huh?"

Vivian frowned, sensing something in his voice. Did he suspect? Hell, did he know? "Short one. Drink some coffee, get energized," she said.

"Hey, coffee sounds necessary," Darvin said. He wiped his palms down the front of his stained pants.

"I also have to change my tampon," Vivian said, surprising even herself. It was the one thing that would give her space in the situation, but she'd meant to mentally weigh a few options, not blurt it out.

"Ahh," Nate said, cringing a hair, as if that explained something.

"What?" Vivian said, suddenly on the offensive, ready to defend the period she wasn't having.

Darvin and Davi laughed, and Tim said, "You done it now."

"I just meant, you're, uh…a little off," Nate said. "I mean, periods make women emotional, right?"

Darvin whistled a sound fantastically close to when Wile E. Coyote stepped off a cliff while holding an anvil. Davi finished it off with a crash noise and clapped hands.

"Think we should get coffee," Tim said, and the laborers scurried off, holding back giggles.

Vivian eyed Nate hard an extra second before remembering this was a ruse and she was so far in the wrong that they ought to build a plank and make her walk it. "I'll let it slide because what do gays know about periods?"

Nate opened his mouth as if to rebuff but stopped himself. "Yeah, sorry. It's just, my mother, she…"

Vivian huffed. She started away without another word. Once from eyeline, she began jogging toward her cabin. She'd be damned lucky if the coke would last three more days. What she'd done? That was insanity and the only way to deal with insanity was to medicate it.

16

"Okay, new plan," Maurice had said after listening to Anna's theory—one that had proved to be most likely correct, "we scavenge all the good stuff and try to recoup some of the losses."

He meant his losses and they all knew it and frowned about the extra work, stuff not written into their contracts. He caught this and made an addendum to his statement.

"Every member will get a bonus, if this stuff's worth anything," he said. "Remember, you're still on company time."

They worked slowly and carefully, removing the weapons while staying clear of the cartons of straw and most likely housed bombs or grenades or mines. They carted away equipment and protective gear, mindful of condition—if stuff was collectable, it was most collectable if it looked new. They tried the light switches and found the water wheels and the batteries they'd been connected to had continued to collect power. The radios worked, but were so heavy they had to find a wheelbarrow to move them. After five hours, everyone was sweaty and dirty, and they'd scavenged enough stuff that it would take a half dozen trips or more to cart it back to the ship.

They took the helmets and rifles on the first trip—sixty of each. Maurice patted them with the hand not steering the outboard motor. "I know a guy who's big in the collecting scene. Think Nazi stuff is more valuable, and World War One stuff, but I'm betting there's not much of this left."

"You mean after America destroyed half their country?" Anna said. She was tired and irritated. The blisters on her hands had reopened and all day it had felt as if someone was watching; that feeling she got when an old man was leering across the gym while she did jumping jacks or yoga. That feeling that had no tangible way to prove but knew to be real no matter what.

"That, and just how old it is. Stuff like this got melted down after the war because losing the fight meant more than lost lives," Maurice said, calling it out over the splashing cut against the waves and the groan of the Evinrude.

Once up tight to the pulley system, Maurice killed the engine and the crew collectively guided the boat over the basket-like system. He grabbed the walkie-talkie from one of the boat's affixed packs and called up. They had to wait only two minutes before Aaron leaned over the side and the boat began rising. All had their heads craned to watch the pulley lines and the darkening skies beyond.

After the huge blow to morale, finding all that interesting stuff set off a strong uptake in mood. All doubted it would last long, but for now, things were going well, all things considered.

"Your wife was on the shortwave, and I told her we blew the engines. She said she'd try you again at seven and then seven-thirty," Aaron said once the winch ceased its activity.

Maurice climbed out first as he was at the back where the stepstool sat. "How's that coming? The engines?" he said as he looked at his watch; five minutes until Jane would be back on the radio.

"They have one engine out and in a spare cabin. Total mess—what's all that?" Aaron nodded at the rifles and helmets.

"That's maybe how we all get a little bonus, after we cover some losses." Maurice had insurance for some of the issues, but getting monies owed from insurance companies wasn't always quick or simple. If an insurance company could point a finger at a culprit and say, 'they owe, not us,' no amount of regularly paid premiums would cover them, even if Maurice never saw a dime from the accused culprit.

"Do they fire?" Aaron said.

"No idea and I don't want anyone testing them on my watch. Might blow to pieces," Maurice said. "Okay, let's get this stuff downstairs. We have any empty containers onboard?"

"No," Michael said.

"Hmm, okay. Let's say they go in with the engine in the spare cabin then. Just have to hope we don't get any surprise inspections. This all probably legally belongs to the Japanese government," Maurice said. "Which cabin?"

Aaron explained and everyone got busy while Maurice hurried to the bridge and the shortwave radio. The moment he crossed the threshold inside, he heard Jane's voice.

"Come in, Chances Taken," she said.

Maurice snatched up the mic. "Here, over."

"Hear you're having some trouble, over," Jane said, her voice suggested she was more accepting than anything else. Nothing she could do to help. Nothing to be mad at. Nothing to get sad over.

"Yeah, but we're near an island absolutely loaded with World War Two junk. Japanese stuff, all abandoned. Very interesting. I'll get Anna to take pictures, over," Maurice said.

"Wow, so maybe this is a blessing in disguise? Over," Jane said.

Maurice sighed, bouncing his head left right, right left and back again. "More likely just won't lose my shirt on the trip. Those engines…shit, they'll need rebuilt. I'm just hoping Viv and Nate can limp us to port and back home, over."

"Yeah, over," Jane said.

"Better get moving. Talk tomorrow, over and out," Maurice said.

"Bye, love you," Jane said.

"Love you too," Maurice said and cradled the mic. He inhaled a deep breath as he stretched his back. This was going to be one very long and very agitating trip…and he really knew only a piece of the trouble he and the crew would soon face.

17

The crew was worn out and showing it until Maurice piped up that most of them would stay put on the island while Antoine, Syl, and himself returned to the ship and offloaded the items, bringing back with them the ingredients for a campfire.

"Well, all right," Tess said.

"Guess we ought to gather some wood?" Anna said.

"Do what you like, I'm taking a break," Tess said and stretched out on the sand, eyes closed to the fast-approaching sundown.

"Good idea," Lavell said.

"Best not stray too far," Michael said. He still held the rifle, though not in a way that suggested he was aching to use it, more like he didn't want to get it sandy. "Maybe each pick a direction and come back with an armload. Shout and I'll come."

Gretchen and Lavell went off behind the southernmost buildings, though not exactly together. Anna went to the northernmost building, which proved to be a shed full of ancient MREs in tin containers and medical supplies in faded cardboard cartons. The sand thickened once into the trees, and she scanned the forest floor for easy access burnable debris. What was there wasn't like what she'd find at home, but guessed fronds burned well enough. She began piling.

The day had been hot work and even now in the dimming light, sweat rolled down the hollow of her throat to between her breasts. She wore a thin tee with short sleeves and the bottom tied above her midriff. Her shorts reached a couple inches below her butt. She had on bikini bottoms beneath and off and on throughout the day considered stripping down and cooling off in the ocean.

Once she had a goodly pile of fronds, she bent at the waist to scoop them up. Something moved behind her, swishing the thick foliage. She spun and scanned the greens, browns, and yellows. No eyes, no likely shapes, no nothing. She was alone, but felt an intense gaze upon her, drinking her in. She shook it off and bent again, reassuring herself mentally that there was nothing to worry about, they'd been on the island all day and hadn't seen a trace of anything untoward. Probably it was some mental defect of suddenly being single when she didn't want to be. A ghost of love imagining Terry behind her perhaps, his arms spread and the world's grandest apology on his lips.

"Yeah right," she whispered and crouched lower to grab an escapee frond from the bottom of the pile. She straightened and again heard swishing behind her. This time she didn't look behind her, instead took off, sprinting until she felt loose beach beneath her feet because what she'd just now heard wasn't imaginary.

She slowed as her heels began slipping in the white, white sand. She glanced back, and when she saw nothing unusual, tried to walk calmly to where the crew was gathering things on the beach. Her heart rate slowed and the sight of Lavell with a hatchet and much of a dead palm tree changed the channel in her brain—because it had to be her imagination.

The hatchet bit into the wood with great success, sending long-dried chunks and chips airborne. After five good strikes, two feet of trunk separated, revealing ant-ridden innards. No surprise. He kept at it and Gretchen occasionally plucked ants from his shoulders and neck.

Anna was happy for her friend, and even a little jealous. Getting rid of Terry was tough but right. She felt unloved, unseen by the opposite sex—the men on the ship were all wise enough to know she was a forbidden treasure, and one not worth the risk— unaware that four real sets of eyes spied her specifically from the forest beyond the fairground.

As it had been on many days in class and nights at bars, she was the subject of fascination above all others in the vicinity.

18

Antoine gathered up sausages, buns, fixins, and the single bag of marshmallows they had onboard. Syl was in the walk-in grabbing two flats of Budweiser cans and a couple bottles of Appleton Estate rum. Maurice, meanwhile, was on his final hurried trek with an armload of scavenged military junk. The trip was a real mess, but it was possible, there was a thread of hope at least, that he'd come out close to even. Losing, at minimum, what he should've earned on the trip was a given.

He set the cases of MRE tins down and swiped sweat from his brow. The guys would be done before him, but instead of hurrying up to the lifeboat, he detoured to the engine room. The laborers and engineers had the two bad engines out and had just begun removing the headers of the third when Maurice had ordered them off to shower. They'd have to work a little longer tonight, once they returned from the beach. Unless they were totally done in. It never paid to force labor beyond extreme expectations, he'd seen that himself in the years before he ever became a captain.

So many didn't realize it; being in charge meant a lot more than being the one who took the largest cut and took the greatest risk. It was about sustainability and leaving a positive mark on those below in the ranks.

He bent to get a better look at the damage to the third engine. The Chances Taken had been so reliable, so much so that he'd felt the weight of impending trouble since the first sailing. He smiled thinking about it, at how green he'd been. Pushing upright, his knees crunched and he suspected he'd been in the engine room longer than he meant to be.

He hurried up the steel steps to the deck to find all awaiting him. They stood around the lifeboat. "What a day, huh?" he said and made a motion with his hand for them to climb aboard. "I'd say it's just about beer o'clock."

As Antoine worked the mechanical box, they began to lower. The rope ladder had already been tossed over the side for when they returned to the ship. Someone would have to climb, probably Aaron; he'd be the first to collect any and all available brownie points on offer.

They touched down, and Davi said through a yawn, "We doing more tonight?"

"How you feeling? Be better to do extra tonight or get an early start?" Maurice said.

The laborers looked at each other and then to the engineers.

"I'll keep at it, nothing intensive in what we have to do," Nate said.

Maurice nodded to him and shifted his gaze to Vivian a moment before he fired up the engine. She'd been heading downhill a while and he couldn't quite pin how or why. Nate on the other hand seemed to be gunning for the chief engineer spot. Almost certainly, he'd have to give it to him, or really get through to Vivian.

"How you feeling?" he said to her, nearly shouting over the buzz of the Evinrude.

"Good. Fine. Okay," she said, snapping the words

off as if startled awake.

Maurice only nodded and they continued enroute to the bright flames dancing through the darkness on the beach. A little fun to waylay the anxiety and effort.

19

The laborers retired to the ship when Maurice, Aaron, and Tess did, only two hours after arriving back on the beach. Nate also left so as to continue dismantling the complicated engine; the sooner the ship got moving, the better. The rest of the crew remained on the beach, acting as if nothing was wrong, tasting the rum and beer while charring marshmallows on sticks. The flames had settled into a comfortable height, one that was easily maintained and managed. Sparks lit on air, and now and then a crewmember had to shuffle away. Regularly someone had to go into the forest and grab more fronds and wood. Gretchen and Lavell had gone together a couple times, stopping along the way for the kind of make-out sessions that made their heads light and butterflies flutter in their guts.

After the third hour had passed, and with the rum in her, Gretchen was downright horny. "Probably should grab some more stuff to burn," she said, despite that the pile next to the fire was big enough to last at least another half-hour, likely longer.

"I'll help," Lavell said, rising behind her and slipping a hand into the back pocket of her shorts.

"After you're done, we'll probably actually need more wood," Michael said, grinning.

"We're getting wood," Gretchen said, a touch on the defensive.

Nobody was fooled by the ruse, but that didn't make it any less necessary. Gretchen picked up pace once out of the fire light and scurried into the bunkhouse, shining a flashlight briefly to find her way through the doorway. The mattresses were all rotten, so Gretchen veered to the wash counter at the far end of the room.

"Bend me over and fuck me," she said into Lavell's neck after he pressed against her.

Her button popped and the zipper came down. His hand dipped into her open shorts. Two fingers swirled that lovely little nub hidden within the hot folds of her pussy. He worked his fingers faster and cradled her ass with his other hand while he sucked her face.

"You want me to fuck you?" he said, panting.

Gretchen had his fly open and was stroking him. She wasn't as skilled and the friction was without lubricant, she worried the labor calluses on her palms might be rug-burning him some, though she didn't slow. She'd given him head two nights in a row and he'd returned the favor once. They hadn't taken it further than that.

She pushed him away and started to turn to lean on the counter, but stopped. "Do you have a rubber?" she whispered.

He'd kept one hand in her shorts and the other on her backside, caressing her ass and working his fingers, saying nothing.

"Do you?" she said.

He remained silent aside from heavy breathing. The wet gushing sounds and the jingle of steel buttons and unzipped flies played soundtrack to the scene.

Gretchen slipped her shorts and panties down her thick thighs. "I don't care," she said, though she did care and knew she'd care a lot more the moment the deed was done. She turned then.

"I'll pull out," Lavell said.

Once she poked out to him, he pressed his hard cock against her ass cheeks. They were cold. He bent her at the waist, and she reached between her legs to guide him inside her pussy. She gasped as he thrust into her a moment after she'd put him on the doorstep. He pumped hard, pressing his abdomen against her back, teasing her nipples as he did so. The clapping sound of their genitals seemed to ring out like an audience enjoying dancers performing the Tropak.

None from the fire heard it.

It did not go unheard, however.

"You dick is so-oh-oh good," Gretchen said, whining.

"Take it. Take it," Lavell said.

"Give it to me," Gretchen said.

Lavell did and did and did. And so well that Gretchen felt fluids creeping down her thighs and Lavell wasn't yet slowing, hadn't yet clenched and quivered and sent that throbbing pulse through her body—because never did she believe he'd pull out. This was nothing like the sex she'd had in college, lightyears from what had happened on prom night with a boy named Joseph Johnson who'd lasted all over three minutes and had a prick like a pencil nub.

Then it happened. Lavell's hands left her breasts and tightened around her shoulders. He stiffened everywhere and seemed to be reeling himself out, as if he was going to do as promised. Gretchen slammed hard against him.

"I want to feel you cum inside me," she said.

"You sure?" he said.

"Fucking do it." Gretchen pistoned herself, bouncing hard against his firm stance.

"I'm cumming," he said, the word riding a hiss.

"God," Gretchen said through a moan.

Lavell's body became a plank and he squeezed into

her, sending every ounce of focus into the chemical act. He crumpled then, leaning down over her, sweaty and spent. He was breathing hard, and Gretchen was breathing almost as hard. As their pulses slowed, so did their breathing, and yet, the panting continued.

Lavell jerked upright, spinning and reaching for the shorts that had puddled at the ankles of his leather boots. Gretchen bent to snatch up hers as well, feeling the cool oozing fluid slip further down her thighs.

"Who's there?" Lavell said.

Gretchen felt around the dark for the flashlight and clicked it on, spinning as she did so. The beam fell on two massive beasts coated in brown fur. They were vaguely humanoid, had large heads and long, clawed fingers. They were on the floor two feet away, humping.

"What the fuck?" Lavell said, breathy as a promise made in the backseat of a convertible parked on Lover's Lane.

The beasts had learned from their parents and their parents had learned from their parents, going all the way back to a female Neanderthal who had raised the world's first sasquatch children. She'd learned to mimic the humans from her parents, and now her furry offspring would carry that tradition on forever. They also carried the engrained knowledge of delicious Mammalia food sources.

The sasquatches had no shorts to pull up and leapt. Survival demanded secrecy and these humans had seen them. The female latched onto Lavell and sank her teeth into his throat before he could cry out. The male leapt onto Gretchen, burying her face in the pelt of his belly as his claws carved into her scalp and skull. In seconds, her brain spilled from the pan and slipped across the pocked cement floor. The male sasquatch leaned out and sucked it up like a Jell-O cube. The female saved the brain for last and feasted upon

Lavell's muscled shoulders and back to start.

After enjoying the choicest morsels, the beasts quietly dragged the corpses out into the forest for their brethren and offspring to consume.

1945 CE

The ship left a hidden port at Kochi at five to eleven in the morning, on its way to the ruse island. They'd received a distress call two nights earlier and it had taken that long for the brass to make up their minds about what to do. The public had become weary with fighting and all expendable or trimmable budgets were being severed at the edges, no matter how necessary.

"I'm not impressed," the captain said to his chief engineer on the bridge. "My son, he turns six in two days and I was this close," he pinched two fingers to about a centimeter apart, "to being there."

"Shame."

"Now we won't be home for weeks, at least. Today is the sixth, count it, maybe the twenty-ninth, maybe thirtieth—"

A blast rocked the words from the captain's mouth. Seconds later, a great backdraft plowed through the windows of the ship, sending the glass shards out like spearheads. The captain and all the crew within the bridge stumbled back, eyes locked on the blooming mushroom of smoke rising from their homeland.

They made it no further and the island was forgotten.

20

Anna had watched her friend go off into the darkness, saw the flashlight beam light in one of the old buildings before shutting down quickly, and felt an intense jealousy. And sadness. She hadn't been single since the ninth grade. She turned to face the fire.

"Marshmallow?" Antoine said, standing over her with the bag of semi-crusty treats.

"I guess," Anna said and accepted one. She'd had a few sips of rum and had to keep herself from getting drunk, because if she got drunk, she might get the kind of emotional that would have the crew talking. She crawled to the edge of the fire where the straightened coat hangers they'd used rested on rocks that represented the fire's perimeter. At first they'd used sticks, but Tess tapped her head and ran to the bunkhouse, returning with a dozen hangers.

Anna held the end over the fire a few seconds to burn away any hotdog or marshmallow residue before sliding her fresh marshmallow on.

"Why do you think they just left this place?" Syl asked, slurring a bit. Next to him was an open bottle of rum and six empty beer cans.

"Who knows," Vivian said, and then sniffled. "Ah, allergies."

Nobody said much to that, she'd been sniffling all night and once, after returning from a pee, Anna was certain the woman had coke on the edge of her nostril but decided it had to be sand. The next time she looked, it was gone.

"I didn't get to look around, can I bum a flashlight?" Vivian said. "Probably be stuck in the engine room for the next two days."

Syl grabbed the one he'd brought from the lifeboat and tossed it into the sand by Vivian's feet. She bent and grabbed it, clicked it on, shooting a strong yellowy beam.

"Thanks," Vivian said.

Anna watched Vivian a moment. She entered one building and left it quickly, starting off for the next building.

"You on fire," Antoine said.

Anna looked at her marshmallow and quickly brought it close enough to her face to blow out the flame. She tried to peel the gooey body off whole, but it had gone too far and she lost more than half as the innards clung to the stick.

"It's all like World War Two stuff, right? Could be the nukes stopped them?" Syl said, letting the suggestion and question hang for anyone to pluck.

Nobody wanted the conversation.

"Another?" Antoine said, holding the marshmallow bag toward Anna. He'd been pacing, alternately sipping beer and rum.

"Thanks," Anna said.

This time she'd do it right; get the hanger red hot at the tip before sliding the marshmallow on. Vivian returned and sat down gently a few feet from Anna, a little bit from where the fire light would cover her wholly. It appeared she'd stuffed the pockets of her shorts and hoodie with something, but like the coke residue, this seemed unlikely.

The marshmallow went grey, and Anna pulled back the hanger. She tapped the hot and crispy edges to be sure it was cool enough before snatching the marshmallow off in a quick and successful pull.

"Très bien," Antoine said. All night he'd done perfect marshmallows whereas the rest of them had to get lucky.

"Probably we should head back to the ship?" Vivian said.

"Yeah," Antoine said. "Where Lavell and Gretchen run off?"

"The bunkhouse," Anna said, speaking around a mouthful of white goo.

"Ree-roo ree-roo," Syl said, mimicking a squeaky bedframe.

"Maybe you go give a shout that we go back to the ship now," Antoine said.

Anna set the coat hanger down next to the flames and pushed to her feet. She brushed off her butt before reaching into her pocket for the keychain penlight she'd grabbed from her purse prior to returning to the island. Syl and Antoine began collecting empties, though the assumption was that they'd be back at least once more before continuing on their course. Vivian seemed to be making like she was busy without doing much of anything. Michael had fallen asleep next to the fire but was awake and blinking at the activity around him.

The voices of her fellow crewmembers thinned to a rumble as Anna made space between her and the fire. She tried to listen for sex sounds or whispered voices. She heard neither.

"Gretchen?" she said, hissing it in a loud whisper.

She reached the doorway and shined her light deeper inside. She saw the beds; all was as it had been before. Anna stepped through the doorway and her foot slipped forward. She shined her light on the floor. The bloody streaks reflected the light's beam like an old man's warning from a slasher flick: *you're doomed if ya stay, this place's got a death curse!*

"Gretchen?" she said, louder now. "Gretchen!"

Anna charged into the bunkhouse, following the blood. There was so, so much of it. A shiver ran through her veins, carting along fatigue and terror.

"Somebody, hel—!"

Anna got no more out before huge furry hands clamped down over her face and waist. She tilted. The flashlight fell from her grip. Her legs kicked wildly and her hands made fists. She punched at this horrible creature that had her as it raced them through the pitch-black forest. And the stink. She couldn't breathe, but the scent was full and everywhere. It made her gag. Distantly, she heard the calls of the rest of the crew on the island.

The sounds were slow and the distance from them to her was increasing by the half-second. The fright and adrenalin and lack of oxygen mingled into a cocktail that put her out less than a minute after being captured. In a clearing, surrounded by trees that had been molded into a high wall over decades, and beneath a thick canopy of fronds, the beast that grabbed Anna sat her down in the sand at the foot of a great stone altar. Grunts and gasps surrounded her sleepy form. The beast that caught her gestured wildly up to the altar, grunting and then spinning. It pointed over and over, grabbing moonlit eye-contact with each of its brethren, including the tykes too small and ignorant to process much and the elderly that were too old and frail to hunt or gather.

The beasts, all thirteen of them, locked arms in a circle. They jumped in unison, grunting a tune almost as old as mankind itself. They began spinning, their feet kicking up sand, dirtying the delicious meat that had been brought back to a hidden homeplace previous to the capture of this sleeping girl.

What was happening now had never happened before.

Anna came to, blinking five times before registering the beastly sounds and the motion around her. She popped to her knees, looked up at the altar, and screamed.

21

They'd searched until the reality of the blood hit them. Michael carried a rifle, but was that enough? Was it nearly enough? On the lifeboat and to the ship. Maurice was on top waiting when the boat rose on the pulley system.

"What do you mean something took her?" he said, wide-eyed and pale beneath the quarter of moon shining down upon them.

Michael explained and Antoine added details and emphasis. Mostly, they focused on the blood in the bunkhouse and that nobody heard a peep. Maurice then tried to climb into the lifeboat. Antoine held him in a bear hug.

"Too dark. Can't see," he said. "That blood was maybe not her blood."

This gave Maurice pause and he lowered the leg he'd lifted to begin up the stepladder into the lifeboat. All besides Antoine and Maurice retired to their cabins. On the bridge, the two men stood in near silence, watching the gentle ocean. Aside from the engine and now this situation, the setting had accommodated their trip; of course that could change at any moment. It took only minutes for gale force winds to envelop the ship.

"You ought to get some sleep?" Maurice said,

making it a question.

Antoine tapped a finger between a few switches on the dash panel. "No," he said.

"Got about four hours until sun-up. Get some sleep," Maurice said, turning to face the man who'd been with him for decades.

"No," Antoine said.

Maurice grabbed his shoulder. "Try. I'll be dead tired and I need you to have energy...I can't sleep, so you have to sleep."

Antoine sighed.

"Just try, for a few hours," Maurice said, his eyes glistening with unshed tears.

"Fine." Antoine started toward the doorway and stopped a step prior to reaching the hall. He spoke over his shoulder. "We will find her. That blood was cold, all sticky."

Maurice inhaled deeply and nodded, though he didn't really believe it. But if Anna was dead, something was going to pay.

22

The list of possibilities seemed both short and endless; what kind of animal lived on the island? Was it an animal at all? Had to be or wouldn't it have left more proof of existence with the things the Japanese military had left behind? Who knew?

The first thought was a cat of some kind, but that didn't really track. It had to be an omnivore. So, a bear, maybe?

"Shit," Maurice said and rubbed his face.

He left the bridge and went down to the cabin where they'd stashed the rifles. The ammunition in boxes appeared old and smoky, probably wouldn't even fire. He had to try. They needed more than two rifles. If there was a maneater, they needed protection from it.

He put a box of cartridges in his pocket and grabbed three rifles. On the bow of the ship, he wedged the rifles between the railing and guard. He jogged away, pants jingling a note on the death song with each pendulous step as his heavy pocket swayed to-and-fro. Outside the door to the mid-deck hallway, he stopped and grabbed a coil of white nylon rope. Once returned, the rope went over the trigger of the first rifle. Maurice then loaded a single smoggy-looking round into the chamber and slammed the bolt. He backed up ten feet, and then five more. He hesitated only long enough to think of Anna before yanking the rope.

Click.

The un-shot round was nearly as loud as a shot round. Maurice sighed and went to check the rifle. The round had fired, sort of. It appeared jammed deep in the barrel. Of course, the weapons were dry and the ammo was dry.

He ran downstairs to the engine room for a container of spent oil—the engines with the ruined blocks were out and the third one was just about stripped to block. On the bow, he dribbled oil into the barrel of the second rifle while he tried to think of something he had on-hand to act as a pipe cleaner. The image of roasting marshmallows came to mind and he broke into a jog once more, heading for a maintenance closet where he kept a spool of thin wire. He'd tear a chunk of shirt free, tie it to the end, oil it, and pull it along the barrel.

Six minutes after imagining the plan, it was done with the second rifle. He stood back fifteen feet and yanked the rope.

Pew.

It was a weaker than expected ejection. Perhaps that was all they'd get. He pulled the ammo box from his pocket and inspected each cylinder. No two were marred at the same level and he withdrew the shiniest of the bunch and set it aside. He removed the round from the third rifle and set to greasing it.

Standing back fifteen feet, rope in hand, he pulled.

Pop!

The echo danced distantly over the waves and through the sky. Maurice nodded, let himself feel excited for two heartbeats before returning his thoughts to Anna. He ran back downstairs to grab more rifles and more ammo.

By the time the sun was up, he'd found the eleven

most functional rifles and the four hundred prettiest rounds. Everything was greased and ready and they'd have army guns instead of slow-going hunting rifles. He wasn't sure everyone would be willing to carry such a rifle, even guessed a couple might want to stay onboard. They could choose that route, they could choose to be unemployed and finding their own way home, too.

Aaron reached the bow first; he was dressed for action: cargo shorts, black tank top, and his steel toed boots. In his hands were two cups of coffee. Not everybody knew Anna had gone missing.

"Want me to sound the horn?" Aaron said, handing off a coffee mug.

Maurice nodded once, tired eyes gazing out at the waves reflecting a pink, pink sun. "Red sky at morning, sailor's warning," he mumbled after Aaron had run off.

Seconds later, the airhorn sounded and Maurice spilled half his coffee onto his hand, jarred by the loud blast that was impossible to get totally numb to.

"Red sky nothing. I'm coming, Anna," Maurice whispered and then shouted, "I'm coming, Anna!"

"Captain?" Tim said. He was in his boxer shorts and bare feet.

Maurice turned. "There's something on the island. Supposing how it looked is correct, it killed Lavell and Gretchen, and carted Anna off. Get dressed. We're going hunting."

23

Vivian looked around at the others. She held a heavy, greasy rifle in her numb hands. She was nearly out of cocaine but had found enough morphine to forget those woes. She'd assumed she'd be tinkering in the engine room all day and shot what she thought seemed like a reasonable amount, a piddly amount. Turned out morphine was a little dab'll do ya kind of high and she was walking around in a pudding bowl, each wriggle a little massage to her veins.

Coke was good.

Morphine was better.

Though it made her slow and disconnected, she found herself grasping at threads of reality, clutching at words spoken by others in the group. The only really clear thought she'd had since Maurice announced that they'd break off into groups was *why do I risk my life to find your kid?* Even stoned, the logic of them separating made no sense when the rest of the crew could survive just fine if they stayed on the boat, fixed the engine, and fucked off to civilization. If Maurice wanted to find Anna, let him. If Lavell and Gretchen were truly dead then none of this was even close to being worth the risk.

Then they were bouncing on the waves, cutting the

lifeboat over the ocean, and she was blinking through long gaps. She nodded when spoken to and followed the set of feet ahead of her. She found herself in a group with Nate, Syl, and Michael. They stopped frequently to examine broken tree limbs and footprints in the sand. They'd moved south—south?—from the bloody bunkhouse, into the thick forest and so far had only confirmed that whatever lived on the island was heavy with large feet.

"An ape, maybe? What do you think?" Michael said, bending down to where Vivian was gazing.

She of course saw nothing special about the sand. Could only blink and nod, suck back drool that kept creeping from her mouth.

"You okay?" Michael said.

Vivian inhaled deeply through her nose and adjusted, focused on the man by her feet. A voice, almost certainly God's, told her what to say and she repeated it flawlessly, though slowly. "I packed Tylenol and I packed codeine Tylenol. My back was sore and I took four of the wrong one. Sorry," Vivian said.

"What about the rest of the days?" Nate whispered.

"Maybe you ought to go back to the beach and wait by the lifeboat," Syl said.

Vivian turned. The forest was thick. How many hours had they been bushwhacking? Dear, Lord, she'd get lost.

"You think?" she said.

"You're toast, you'd better," Syl said.

"How?" she said.

"Holy, you sure it was just codeine?" Michael said.
She nodded.

"Look," Syl said and took her arm in his left hand. He pointed with his right to about twenty feet away. "There's the roof of the bunkhouse. Don't lose sight of it. You'll be back on the beach in five minutes."

Five minutes? They'd been out for so, so long—her

veins…the blood was good to her veins when she moved and she closed her eyes. Her feet began to move faster and she dropped the heavy, oily rifle she carried. Voices rose behind her. They were underwater, sinking in quicksand, coming from a broken radio while she floated in a cloud.

Vivian walked until the trees disappeared around her and the bunkhouse was behind her. She took a dozen more staggering steps to the beach and then lay face-first in the golden sand. Each grain played against the tiny hairs of her body like fingers to instrument strings, and she writhed in tune with the beautiful music of the wind though her body remained still in the warm morning light.

It would be close to two hours before she fished the strange morphine inhaler tube from her pocket to rejuvenate her high, not a clear thought in her head.

24

The southbound group reached another swatch of beach three hours after sending Vivian away. Nate hadn't been able to hold his tongue any longer. "She's totally fucked," he said and then went on to suggest Vivian was a coke addict, said he'd seen powder in and around her nostrils. He called her unprofessional and dangerous. Finally, after he'd said all that he was mostly certain about, he said what he knew to be true in his gut, despite no real evidence to support the fact. "I think she sabotaged the engines."

"What?" Michael said, stopping and lowering his rifle.

"Serious," Nate said.

"That's crazy," Michael said.

They stood a moment beneath the late morning sun, sweaty and hot. They came to an agreement without broaching it verbally: break time. Each rested a Japanese rifle against their legs and sipped water from liter jugs they'd brought along. Syl pulled snacks out of his packs and was eating a donut that had been vacuum-sealed, while simultaneously smoking a cigarette.

"Wouldn't surprise me," Syl said. "I had a cousin who was a junkie. He got mad at his mom and burned down their house. He didn't remember why after he did it. Did a year in the hospital and then a year in jail; I guess in case he was faking it."

Michael shook his head slowly, eyes pinned on the waves washing ashore, his nose drinking in the fresh, untouched scent of that literal piece of nowhere. "How long until the engines are back up? Once we find Anna."

"Think we'll find her?" Syl said.

"Maybe eight, nine hours," Nate said. "Then we'll want to let the cement set in the block, otherwise, a bit of pressure for a little while and *boom!*"

Michael tilted his chin some and let the breeze play through his hair. "I hope we aren't doing this again tomorrow. Feel that wind? Any second something might blow in on top of us. With one and a half engines, I don't think we'll want to fight with a storm."

"Won't be much fight. Just take a beating and hope for the best," Nate said.

"Gotta shit," Syl said and started back toward the tree line with his rifle and pack. They'd cut all the way through the thick forest and discovered another beach.

Nate and Michael both watched him leave. There wasn't much else to say about the engines or the weather without getting into a fuss about it. Seemed as if they had problems enough without considering further ill luck.

"You think Lavell and Gretchen are dead?" Michael said.

"Was a lot of blood," Nate said.

"Like maybe enough that it was also Anna's blood?" Michael said, left eyebrow upturned.

Nate tilted his head and then took another mouthful of water. He nearly spat when Syl's voice rang out with terrified desperation written all over its tone. A rifle shot echoed then. Followed by a second shot and a second scream. Nate scooped his rifle and shouldered his pack after slipping the water bottle away. Michael was ahead of him, rifle aimed and pack on.

The shade next to the beach was enough of a light change that both men had to slow drastically. Blinking into the dimness, Syl's location wasn't immediately known. He screamed again and both heads snapped around to their left and saw their crewmate flying through the air, his legs pedaling at the emptiness and his arms bent at hideous angles. Nate and Michael had to jump back to avoid being struck.

Michael saw what Nate hadn't and opened fire at the massive thing that had thrown Syl. The fire shot blasted from the rifle and flew, true to the loose aim of its operator. The round nailed a furry hip of an eight-foot-tall beast with humanoid features and an extended and cone-shaped cranium. The second squeeze of the trigger was not so fortunate. The round caught somewhere along the way and lodged in the barrel.

A second beast rose and grunted as the first beast fell to its fours with a throaty groan. This second one charged at them and Nate aimed.

"Jesus fuck—!"

He got nothing more out as Michael squeezed the trigger again and a good round nailed the one still in the barrel, sending shrapnel out like a party popper as the old steel burst. Nate took a sliver through the right eyeball. He fell to his knees and immediately put his hands to his face after dropping his weapon, inadvertently slamming the sliver deeper, cracking the bone at the base of the socket. His wail was incredible. It sent birds airborne.

Michael's hands were bloody but mostly he was fine. He gave Nate another glance and then the beast coming at him. He spun and ran from the beast, certain, for no good reason, that the ocean would save him from this impossible situation. He made it six sandy steps before a great black flash clouded his vision.

The world came back to him in bits.

Slurp.

Crunch.

Grind.

The great furry hands came at his face, two fingers out. Those fingers had claw-like nails that pressed against his eyes. The beast's other hand wrenched the top of his skull, twisting as if getting into a stiff jar of pickles.

Another black flash came at him like being struck dead on the nose by a fastball, and his final living thought was, *I'm food.*

25

The shots rang loudly enough that all but two crewmembers heard it: Anna and Vivian. Tess, Davi, and Darvin charged toward the shots, and the accompanying shouts, while Maurice, the other two laborers, and Antoine continued down an undeniably trodden path. Whatever it was that lived on the island was big, and it had been there a very, very long time.

"What you think going on?" Antoine whispered.

"I think if the animals are out hunting, we might get lucky and chance upon Anna," Maurice said.

"Man in Russia survived a month in a bear den. He played dead and the bear had him stashed for later. Once he got his wits and the chance, he crawled away," Darvin said.

"I think it's pretty clear they didn't kill Anna, not right away," Maurice said.

Nobody argued it, despite that just because someone says something and wants it to be true, even when they're the captain, it didn't make it true. There was a lot of blood on that bunkhouse floor.

Ahead of the group, a wall of fronds settled in front of the path. Spiderwebs thick enough to catch small, highly colorful birds coated the greenery like dust at a flea market. Antoine took the long knife he'd brought from his kitchen and slashed the way clear, revealing a crystalline watering hole. Everybody stopped a moment. The world was serene and the weather agreeable. In any other circumstance...

"Man, no shots for a bit. Think they got it?" Tim said.

"No," Maurice said. Again, he had no reason to suggest it but was firm in doing so.

A handful of quiet moments mounted into minutes and Darvin stared into his reflection upon the pool's surface. The edges were roughed up and muddy, but otherwise it looked nice. Like something from a brochure selling a tropical paradise. Around the pool were short, leafy plants. In three directions, new trails branched off.

"We should split up," Maurice said.

"You crazy?" Tess said.

Maurice looked at her, frowning heavily.

"I'm not killing myself for you or your daughter. It's bad enough we're out here, but I'm not suicidal," she said.

"Yeah," Darvin said. "I have kids waiting for me at home."

Maurice looked at all the nodding heads and then to Antoine.

"We do smart thing, okay?" he said.

Maurice scrunched up his mouth and wrinkled his forehead as if pained. "Fine, we follow each route; if it doesn't lead to Anna, we double back and try the next one."

The nods continued and Antoine and his long knife led the way to the route heading straight north. None could be all that long and surely one of them went somewhere vital.

26

Anna turned from where she lay, surrounded by beasts—*who you kidding, girl? Fucking sasquatches!*—and saw the frond wall fall as if all the strings had been cut away and the shiny greenery was cascading to the ground like lazy snow. Terry was walking toward her in a black tank top, his muscles taut and shiny with sweat. He carried his father's hunting rifle, aiming at the first beast.

Boom!

The beast crumbled. The others popped to their feet and Terry handled them like a sharpshooter, pegging them in the huge triangular foreheads, one after another. They fell and fell and fell. The blood rode the air like a mist upon the moor and fur flared out like a cat fight.

"Terry!" Anna screamed, holding her arms out to him after he slaughtered the final beast. She knew he still loved her, and she absolutely still loved him. She'd never be alone again, not for a week, a day, not a fucking hour. "I love you so much, Ter-bear."

Terry stooped in, arms wide, but skirted Anna's touch. He picked up the bones that had been on the altar, and held them tight to his chest, their stiff fingers tightening on his back. He leaned in and opened his mouth. The leathery skull with the scalp of stringy brownish grey hair stretched over top like a shower cap opened its bone jaw. It revealed a green, green tongue and Terry writhed his own tongue against it, snakishly.

Anna screamed in her dream, though only moaned in real life. The beasts crowded around her. They watched in rapt fascination. She opened her eyes and saw that her dream, though horrid, was still better than the truth. Her gaze drifted from each face to the next until she settled on the altar. The bones remained in place. Next to the altar was a secondary rising of dirt and sand mixed in with woven frond petals.

One of the beasts dropped to its fours and crawled to this second rising and rubbed the surface while facing Anna. It harbored an expectant expression hinting at the edges of its animalistic face. Another beast from the periphery dropped and crawled up behind Anna, scooping her in its arms before she had a chance to argue the case for remaining in place. She fought before and got nowhere, so now she stiffened and imagined being a doll, like the skeleton was—was that it? A doll?

Anna didn't really think so.

It was more.

The beast set her down on the raised seat next to the skeleton. She went floppy when the beast tried to hoist her and mold her to resemble her boney counterpart. Once Anna got it, she cooperated and the beast touching her with those dirty, stinking hands let her be.

All the beasts drew in close to sit in the sand, as if Anna were about to begin story time. She didn't know what to do, so she did nothing. She sat, posed next to an ages' dead figure, waiting for a miracle.

27

Davi, Tim, and Aaron backtracked in a rush. Though the shots and shouts were much further away, they stopped at the first body they saw—Vivian—who lay on the beach, unresponsive and limp.

"You guys get her into the lifeboat. I'll go on," Aaron said.

Davi and Tim looked at each other, wide-eyed. Tim then shrugged. The laborers bent at the knees, one at Vivian's armpits and the other at her calves.

"Follow me, once you get her secured," Aaron said, calling it over his shoulder.

He continued on, jogging over the thick flora and sandy dirt. This island had seemed so close to perfect, and a lucky break, given what had happened. It was hard to believe it had turned so fully on its head. A damned nightmare in paradise. He slowed as he entered the dim forest, letting his eyes settle to the change of light. There was a scent. Burnt oil and spent matches and…shit. It smelled as if someone had taken a great big—

"Jesus," he said, stopping up, the toes of his boots smooshing into mucky red dirt. "Jesus," he said again, bringing the rifle up and scanning the woods around him.

Everything was calm and motionless aside from the gentle sway of the trees and the occasional bird flying by his radar. Those birds were small, small enough that he didn't bother focusing on them. Whatever had left the meaty mess at his feet was much bigger. A branch cracked to his left, and he spun, his foot skidding deeper into the human muck.

Nothing.

A branch cracked directly behind him and he spun again, both feet now deep in the leftovers of one of the Chances Taken crew. He had no way of telling whom.

Nothing.

A branch overhead snapped and a large frond came crashing down.

"Jesus. Jesus," Aaron mumbled, walking backward, scanning all the greens and browns and greys and wet, wet reds. He saw nothing untoward. His aloneness in the situation finally hit him and he shouted, "Somebody, help!"

He kept walking in reverse, kept scanning, but it was as if it was only he and the birds. Until he heard another snap. This one he felt as well. His weight toppled onto his suddenly broken leg. The jagged end of his right tibia jutted from the bare pinkish meat like a fork prong through a chunk of steak. The rifle was out of his hands as they reached shakily toward the break.

"Help!"

Furry knees pressed down onto his shoulders. A less furry scrotum dangled at the weight of a pair of hefty testicles only an inch from his nose. The scent of this bulky creature was intense and horrible. Sour and animal. He gagged and the animal shifted, as if to gauge this reaction a little closer and Aaron got some air into his lungs.

"Somebod—!"

The beast sat back, silencing him. Aaron gasped to scream again. The beast pressed its ass harder onto his chest, which sent the last of the air from his lungs in a painful whoosh. He squirmed and sucked greedily, but his lungs wouldn't fill. The beast leaned forward, curling in a way that seemed almost human. It pressed its crusty and yet gooey lips to Aaron's face, over his right eye. The terror of uncertainty was almost as bad as—

It sucked.

Aaron tried to scream, tried to thrash and could do neither. The pop. The smoosh. The crunch. The coldness left behind while the stringy red tendrils of viscera reeled up the beast's chin and into its mouth like spaghetti. The beast leaned in again after swallowing and Aaron closed his eye as hard as he could to keep it in his head.

The pressure came.

Pop!

Aaron sucked and gasped for breath and got nowhere. As the beast chewed, it ran a nail deep along Aaron's forehead, so deep he felt it in his teeth. The beast then made a tight fist and punched his forehead twice. Instantly, life no longer belonged to the former first mate of the Chances Taken.

The beast worked quickly, fingering the hole and breaking skull, much like cracking an especially wily eggshell. The beast followed along the gouge line it had cut to snap the bone. It kept at this for close to a minute before it had cleared away enough of the protective bits to get at the sweetest treat of all. It held Aaron's sumptuous brain in its furry hands, blood and slimy pink fluid oozing between its fingers. The beast opened wide and took the entire left side of the man's brain in a single bite. It chewed, leaning back a touch, luxuriating in this prize.

28

Tim and Davi scanned Vivian's body while they carried her. No blood. No bumps. No bruises. She moaned a little, and drool trickled down her cheek to her hair, had done so enough prior to their picking her up that sand had clumped out like cat piss in a litter box. Something was very fishy about this. They set her in the lifeboat and stood back a moment.

"Looks like Aunt Lily," Davi said.

Lily wasn't Davi's aunt, but he knew her well enough. She was a regular party animal at bingo and on weekends at the hotel. She worked reception at the east wing of the hospital where the junkies came for shots and parents took their kids to see the speech pathologist. Everyone in town knew her and knew to leave her be if they saw her taking a 2:00 AM nap on the sidewalk.

"I think she's a cokehead," Tim said.

Davi nodded. "Coke ain't putting her to sleep."

Tim tilted his head, taking the point. Before he could speak, Aaron's voice rang out. Begging for help.

The pair broke into a jog, back up the beach to where they'd left their rifles. Neither had said it but had silently agreed upon only taking risks as far as popping off a few rounds. After that, they'd have to develop a real plan if they were going to run around this foreign landscape. It was plain ignorance to assume that their humanity meant they were on top of the food chain.

Another scream rang out, one painfully short-lived: "Help!"

"Damn," Davi said, the word hissing out on a heavily expelled breath.

It was in no way clear whether they'd come on a rescue mission or a salvage mission. And while the other crewmembers talked about bears, Tim and Davi, as well as Darvin, had been considering something a little more otherworldly. Having a demon or malevolent spirit trapped on an island, perhaps cast off to an island in the times before man, was no crazier than half the stuff in The Bible.

"Somebod—!" Aaron's voice played over the island as if coming from an abruptly unplugged loudspeaker.

They slowed at the edge of the forest and moved carefully, as if tracking a grizzly back home. Ahead, they spotted trampled flora where the trail bent around a coppice of skinny young trees. There were scents aplenty, and at least one of those smells told them to turn back and make for the beach. What kept them going was the sound. The wet smacking and heavy breathing and snorts of enjoyment. These noises mingled into a single harmonious truth: that sound was the sound of something eating a wet, wet meal.

The men ceased their forward motion and began swinging slowly to their right, not quite on the path. They'd done this enough before that they understood how to move without disturbing an otherwise distracted animal. Once around the small trees that had blocked their view, they aimed in unison.

The beast had a mouthful of brain, juices glistening down its furry chin, when it looked up and spotted the crewmembers. Davi and Tim wore bug eyes of surprise. Their heads each played through a rolodex of sasquatch *knowledge*. Their index fingers remained true to the experiences of their lives and the will to get home.

Davi's shot nailed the beast in the forehead.

Tim's shot nailed the beast in the stiff-looking left breast.

It dropped backward with a thump that snapped twigs. A fine red mist hovered over the felled creature. The men were already gone, shooting off like a pair of rockets. They kicked through the beach sand wordlessly, moving as efficiently as was possible, and then climbed into the lifeboat floating by the dock. They ducked from view, rifles hot in their hands, and faced each other.

"Sasquatch?" Davi said.

"Sasquatch," Tim said.

"Think we killed it?" Davi said.

"Think we killed it," Tim said.

"Not alone out here," Davi said, not a question.

"No way, no how," Tim said.

29

Maurice stopped suddenly about a minute after hearing the double shot echo. The thought hit him like the ghost of that paired shots' echo: where the animals were was where Anna had to be. They were looking in the wrong spot!

They'd gone and come back from the first trail, which had led them to a huge fruit bush, one that was plundered but for tiny little berries still weeks from being ripe. This second trail stank. Stank of shit and piss. Multiple times they'd had to sidestep coils and mounds of brown and blue—that blue a shade similar to the berries—feces. Whatever animal lived on the island, it wanted to keep its waste separate from where it ate and drank and likely slept.

"We need to go back. They're finding the animals back there. We need to go back," Maurice said.

None argued. The morning had become afternoon and the toilet trail was baking, infusing the scents of their sweat with all the waste in a way that clung to the crewmembers.

"I need a shower," Tess said when the watering hole came back into view.

"Disgusting," Antoine said. "That stink."

"Yeah," Darvin said, grimacing before taking a

deep, deep breath of fresh air—the waste stench lingered.

Maurice said nothing. He kept the original pace, leading them back the way they'd come. They re-entered the forest briefly. The building again came into view and Maurice upped the tempo, nearly jogging back to the humanized area. When they reached the beach and the scorching sun, Maurice had no choice but to slow, squinting against the brightness—they had to slow anyway to spot the trail Michael's group had followed. By the sound of the distance, it almost certainly had to be Michael's group that had discovered the animal.

"Hoped they'd be here. With animal," Antoine said.

They crossed the beach. It again seemed like a paradise. All that wilderness and greenery and birds chirping and ocean waves lapping. Tess sighed, pausing a moment behind the trio of men leading her.

"Tess."

"Tess."

"Tessssss!"

The voices were loud whispers and didn't fully hit her until it was almost too late. Their foursome had reached the trail and were making toward the forest anew. Tess turned and looked around, then she saw Tim and Davi in the lifeboat, waving their arms.

"Hey!" she said and inadvertently pointed her rifle at the men. "Stop!"

Maurice was the last to do so. He turned, frowning. Darvin and Antoine were looking at the lifeboats and Tess was looking at Maurice.

Darvin wasted no time in consideration and started off toward the beach and then dock.

"Where you going?" Maurice said. He was hellbent on following the panicked whims that entered his head, so much so that he never once questioned a task while he was at it. He saw nothing beyond saving Anna, who he *knew* was alive and who he *knew* was somewhere in or near this particular patch of forest.

"Have to ask them," Antoine said, though didn't take a step away from the captain's side.

"Yeah, what if they have Anna in the boat, injured?" Tess said and started away, distantly trailing Darvin.

"You think?" Maurice said. Tess didn't hear or simply ignored him. He turned to Antoine. "You think?" Straying from his new plan was a difficult notion to swallow.

"Possible, right?" Antoine said and touched Maurice's shoulder, pulling him along.

Quickly, the crewmembers were across the beach and to the dock, their footfalls parading a tune of retreat upon the rusty steel. At first, when Maurice saw the sprawled figure, his heart leapt, thinking it was Anna. When he realized it wasn't, the post euphoria crash made his knees wobble. He leaned against the boat, looking at Vivian's dopey face and thinking he'd like to kill her for simply not being what he wanted to see.

"Sasquatch?" Darvin said, not trace of incredulity in the word.

"It was eating Aaron. He went in after the shots. We thought Vivian was hurt but I think she's high," Tim said.

"Doesn't stink like liquor, has to be high," Davi said.

Tess climbed aboard and lifted Vivian's arm by her wrist. The pulse was normal. "She seems fine. She say anything at all?"

Before either Davi or Tim could answer, Maurice said, "Did you kill the fucking thing?"

"Yeah," Tim said.

"It can't be alone," Davi said. "It would die. I bet it and its friends ate the Japanese."

Darvin's eyes got huge. "Maybe it was Japanese. An experiment."

"So, you saw no signs of Anna?" Maurice said. He stood, ready to get back out there.

"You can't go out there. Not without a plan," Tim said.

"This is home turf, eh? We can't win without a plan," Davi said.

"Did you see any trace of Anna?" Maurice said.

Antoine sighed. "What about others?"

"If the beast got them..." Davi trailed, and Tim shook his head.

"I knew it. I knew we should've checked that third path," Maurice said and punched his thigh with the hand not holding the rifle. "Come on."

Nobody moved a muscle.

"Let's go!" Maurice said, head shaking in minute jerks, his eyes wide as the Pacific Ocean.

Vivian's mouth loosened and then she squinted up before blinking wide. Her pupils were huge and glassy. "I broke the engines," she mumbled. "I'm queen of engine breaking." Her eyes snapped shut.

Silence reigned until Tim said, "We need a plan."

"You really think sasquatches?" Tess said.

"She say she broke the engines?" Davi said.

30

Maurice finally settled down after Antoine started a fire and heated up the steel urn of coffee. Those who smoked sat tapping ashes into the sand, sipping from stubby grey cups. Maurice was on his feet looking out to the ocean and the Chances Taken. It sat like a lone tooth in a gaping mouth, waiting to be plucked before a set of dentures could be fitted.

"If she really broke the engines, she not only jeopardized all our lives, she's responsible for anyone not coming out of the forest," Maurice said.

"Think it possible?" Antoine said.

"Yeah. I knew she was having trouble. I thought it was just booze. Vodka, and then mouthwash the smell away, but coke?" Tess said. "I mean, yeah, I saw some signs, but who guesses, right? Thought I was seeing things."

Maurice dropped to the sand, crossing his legs as he fell. "I have an idea."

"Yes?" Antoine said.

All the rest looked at Maurice's sweaty back. Little bits of greenery clung to his shirt like garnishes.

"We need to know how many…animals there are," Maurice said.

"How do we do that?" Darvin said.

"I ain't going back into the jungle until we get an angle," Tim said and then yawned.

Maurice swiped a hand over his brow. The trickle of sweat ran down his arm, growing larger and larger like a snowball in an avalanche, before streaking to his elbow and dropping into the sand. In that moment, he felt aside from man, as if his humanity was locked up and left behind.

"We make Vivian pay for her crimes," Maurice said.

"What?" Tess said, clear alarm in her voice.

Maurice turned slowly. His face was solemn, free of emotion, and hard as brick. He licked his lips and downturned his chin as if to study his hands, the coffee cup they held. He brought his head up slowly after a sigh. "Bait."

"Bait?" Darvin said.

"Bait?" Tess said.

Antoine nodded. "Bait; draw them out?"

"That's right, we bring the beasts to us. I know, *know* Anna's down that third trail out there. I know it! We bring them away from her and go in to rescue her. Simple," Maurice said. All that emotion that had been vacant was now animated and written clearly upon his face, deep in his tired eyes.

"Are you crazy?" Tess said.

"Not at all," Maurice said. "She's crazy. She's the reason we're here. She deserves whatever happens on this island, and more." Maurice was seething, the muscles of his arms tight, his veins standing out like the docking ropes on the ship. "She won't get hurt unless we all get hurt."

"How the hell do you figure that?" Tess said.

"We set her up and surround her. The animals come and we take them out from the wings. Only if they get us do we not protect her," Maurice said. "It's more than she deserves."

"Listen to yourself! Bait animals with your chief engineer? You've lost it. Look, it sucks the animals got Anna, but they got Aaron and Lavell, Gretchen and probably others, too. You have to face it: there's no proof Anna is out there," Tess said.

The laborers cringed and studied their coffee cups. Antoine shook his head. Maurice stared daggers into Tess.

"I'd know if she was dead. I'd know. I'm her father!" Maurice said.

"You wouldn't, though. You think you would, but that's not how real life works. That's shit from movies and dumb books. Real life doesn't send out signals. The universe is scattered and random. It's not here for us, it's not tethering people. We're all bits to some giant puzzle that doesn't actually fit together," Tess said.

Maurice vibrated then, from the head on down. "That's not true," he said, his voice a harsh bark. "I would know. I'm her father, I would know."

Tess huffed and turned to face the ocean.

Quiet reigned for minutes that passed like cold syrup through a straw. Finally, Antoine said, "What is the plan, Captain?"

Maurice gritted his teeth, nodding. "First, make sure she's good and doped so she doesn't fight, and if they get us and then her, so this doesn't hurt."

At this, Tess turned around again, eyes full of tears. "You've lost it."

31

By the time they had everything planned, Antoine had to fix supper over a campfire. All ate their hotdogs on their way to posts. Long before sundown, all were in position and silent, ready for the inevitable.

Each of the laborers were on a rooftop beneath strategically placed fronds. They had their rifles in front of where they lay, stretched out, aiming in the general vicinity of their bait. Below, semi-buried in sand were Antoine and Tess. Maurice was on the ground, closest to Vivian, hidden behind and beneath a prickly bush with small blue berries aplenty. Vivian was stoned, head lolling where she leaned against the bedframe they'd taken from the bunkhouse and driven into the sand. Her hands were tied loosely to the smoky grey coils. Blood oozed from the nine cuts they'd made in her flesh to loosen the blood scents, and she wore only her underwear and bra. Her cargo shorts, shirt, and boots were a foot away in the sand. In her pockets they'd located shooting morphine, a sniffing tube of morphine, and a small baggy of cocaine. They'd held the tube under her nose for thirty seconds before touching her. She reacted to their hands not at all. They could've used her as a punching bag and she wouldn't have noticed.

The sun loomed redly. The atmosphere cooled a few notches. The moon eventually took over. Maurice crept from hiding to light small, rusty kerosene lamps they'd found in with the military stuff—they didn't seem worthy of carting off the island; kerosene lamps hadn't changed much from then to now. A bit of luck that they hadn't seen value. The flames weren't high enough to enlighten beyond a couple feet, but it would be enough to pick out shapes from the shadows.

The minutes mounted until more than an hour passed. The laborers were especially restless and fidgety. Their locations weren't as comfortable as those in the sand, and they didn't have the same stake as Maurice. Still, they moved little. The scene became a tableau, aside from the flickering flame…and Vivian.

"Hello?" Vivian whispered, her voice raspy as crinkled paper. Her head moved left to right, right to left. She yanked a hand, grunting. "What the hell?" she said, a little less groggy.

From the trees directly before her, a furry foot crept, seemingly weightless in its movements. Maurice waited, waited, waited—the order was to let him fire first—waited, as the beast floated closer. He tightened every muscle but for those in the index finger of his right hand.

32

The sasquatches circled around Anna, who suddenly sat upright and gazed vacantly at the sky, only a moment after a distant, double shot rang out. There'd been other shots, but this was the first they'd reacted to with moans. They didn't speak, not really. Next came the grunts and pointing. All but four of them hurried away from the clearing and the altar with the ancient Neanderthal bones marking the head of the space.

Like practiced cat burglars, the beasts stalked quickly and silently. They cut through the thick foliage and raced for the source of the psychic ping that suggested danger. Normally when they felt this, it was after a deep knowledge of impending misfortune had been at them for days, weeks in some cases. Once before they felt it instantly when one of their own attempted to capture a shark out in the open water. Another time they felt that lasering punch to their psychic insides when a storm blew down a tree, sending the top spiraling into one of their own.

The only other psychic knowledge they ever felt was departure, and none currently alive knew anything of that. It had been centuries since any of their brethren struck out and sought worlds beyond the island.

They reached their fallen brother and circled tightly.

Furry hands touched the hot, stinking body and together they moaned a cry that was something akin to tradition. After a few minutes, the first of the sasquatches withdrew their touch and sought out the other hunters who'd initially gone to harvest the interloper meat.

These two sat at the base of a palm tree, holding hands and humming that tune of commiseration. Tears dampened the fur of their faces, the blood still wet upon their chins and mouths. Their clawed fingernails clogged with entrail meat.

The time had come to take the small things who brought the new female god into their midst more seriously. They knew what to do and acted accordingly. Some of the beasts took to high trees that oversaw the beach and former military instalment. Others waded out into the ocean, silent and low. The rest remained close enough to watch and not be seen—it helped that the interlopers had poor vision when it came to discerning sasquatch from tree, especially as the shadows began stretching.

Hours passed and the sasquatch did as they had learned to do from the wise female Neanderthal who would eventually be seen as their god, the figure whose bones remained upright when many millennia had come and gone: they observed, they considered, they understood, they counter-planned.

33

Maurice did not fire. It was almost as if he'd frozen at the sight of the great creature. Vivian screamed steadily while wriggling free of the ties holding her up before falling into the sand. The beast approaching her remained halfway shrouded in shadows. Maurice waited, watching; something was hinky with how this animal moved. It glided, taking no steps.

"Shoot it!" Tess screamed and popped from her hole.

Maurice saw the rough ends of the trees beneath the beast's armpits as the head came full view, as did the chest. This thing was dead and this was a clever trick by an animal much smarter than they had anticipated.

Shots began ringing out, a few nailing into the already dead beast.

"No!" Maurice shouted and looked back.

Tess was standing, squeezing her trigger, her shots steadily dropping down, down, down. The weight and exertion of firing did her in quickly. Antoine remained where he'd been, though he'd also caught the shooting bug. His rounds were closer, a couple even hit, but none of it mattered a lick. Tess dropped her rifle and spun on her heels, kicking up sand to shoot off as if from runner's blocks. She was making decent ground, too.

Sopping and huge, three beasts were on her long before she could reach the assumed safety of the lifeboat. They'd come from the ocean and flanked the offensive. Tess screamed as furry hands grabbed her head and tightened like a vise while lifting her kicking and swinging body two feet from the sand. Blood oozed along her cheeks and from her ear, sprayed from her screaming mouth. Her eyes bugged like the dagger hands of a Spielberg pirate skeleton. She pissed and shit, everything loose.

The other two beasts made for Antoine in his not-so-hidden hiding spot. He was still firing at the distraction. The closer of the two lifted its big, big foot and stomped Antoine's back hard enough that his tongue sprang far enough free that the frenulum caught between his teeth and tore open while retracting back into his mouth. He screamed nonsense as he gasped, sucking down a great wash of blood and sand. The beast stomped again, using both feet this time. The snapping of ribs sang out nearly as loudly as the shots. His arms rocketed outward to splay loosely on the sand in a very Christ-like pose.

From the rooftops, the laborers began firing on the trio that had emerged from the ocean. These ones glistened beneath the moonlight like sparkling targets. All three of the laborers had experience hunting, so the shots were true to aim, sending great red mist puffs into the tropical air while furballs puffed and spiraled wetly to the sand. The laborers shifted aim quickly, scanning for living, moving beasts.

Too late for Antoine, the beast that had stomped him—now dead—had already sent pieces of bone through numerous vital organs. Too late for Tess, her skull was now a thousand-piece jigsaw puzzle within a meat sack. Too late to come out of this battle unscathed.

Maurice remained where he was and began guessing with his aim. He fired into the trees directly above and to the side of the ruse beast riding the wooden poles. He was rewarded with a pained bestial cry. The dead sasquatch being puppeteered dropped, folding loosely into the sand in an ape-like visage. Enormous, big as the entire universe, two beasts broke from the woods, one was bleeding from the chest. Maurice began rattling off shots at the same time Tim and Davi took aim.

Darvin had lucked out and glanced in Tim's direction. There, directly behind his friend, was a beast about to climb onto the roof where Tim had hidden. Darvin's Spidey Sense clicked in, and he immediately spun, knowing, *knowing* a beast would be behind him as well. His shot couldn't have hit better if he'd aimed. The close-range rifle round bore a hole big enough to sink a putt through a stinking beast's incredible cranium.

"Behind you!" Darvin shouted, his voice cracking at the pitch and desperation within the words.

Tim turned, trusting the advice wholly, and began firing. The third shot hit, but only in the beast's arm, an inch above a meaty elbow. It leapt then and the roof crashed when the weight landed. Together they went down, even as Tim continued squeezing rounds into the monstrous shape.

Maurice was up and looking around. Vivian was on the ground, huddled next to her pants where she searched blindly through the pockets, mumbling, "Bad trip, bad trip." On the two remaining rooftops, Darvin was prodding a sasquatch corpse with the barrel of his rifle. On the other standing rooftop, Davi could not be seen. Furry arms pumped up and down, splashing in a painfully promising blood puddle. There was no way Davi was alive up there, no coming back from that beastly beating. Maurice lifted his rifle and took aim.

He fired twice and the sasquatch pounding the blood puddle tipped sideways and crashed into the low-lying shrubs next to the building.

The island seemed to halt then, as if the world had ceased spinning so that the remaining crewmembers of the Chances Taken might regain their bearings. Smoke rose from hot rifles. The atmosphere reeked of burnt oil and spent ammunition. From his spot inside the caved in building, Tim moaned.

After another quiet thirty seconds, Maurice said, "Who's still kicking?"

34

"How'd they think to do that?" Darvin said. "They're animals. How'd they get so smart?"

Darvin, Tim, and Maurice sat in the sand. Between them were the bodies of their fallen comrades.

"Do what?" Maurice said.

"Know to trick us? That's way smart, with the dead one. How'd they know that they had to trick us?" Darvin said.

Tim shook his head gently. He had taken off his tank top and fashioned a sling for his broken arm.

"Who knows. It gave them away, though. No more underestimating," Maurice said and pulled a jackknife with a four-inch blade from his pocket. "They got us, but we got more of them, and now we know they're smart."

Darvin frowned. "There's only two and half of us left. You want us to go into the bush with just us?"

"No. Tim's staying behind," Maurice said as he pushed to his feet.

"I am?" Tim said.

"You be in the ship and ready when you see us come off the island," Maurice said.

Darvin huffed a big breath that puffed out his cheeks. "Man…"

"Look, I have a plan," Maurice said. "But first, we get the bodies onto the lifeboat, and get Tim in place on the ship. Nate had things ready enough that we can move about a tenth of the speed. We'll ring off distress signals and make as much distance as we can. We know they can swim. We know they can climb."

"Don't want none of that," Darvin said, as if imagining awaking in his cabin to a slobbery sasquatch face looming above him.

"What then?" Tim said. "I mean when I'm waiting."

"We show them what evolution can do. We show them our big old brains," Maurice said. There was a glint of crazy cunning in his expression, one the others would simply have to trust; no turning back now, they'd sacrificed too much to lose this war.

35

Anna sat on her throne, watching the agony unfold within the six remaining sasquatches. It was horrible, like watching apes lose a community elder, but many times over. The shots had ceased ringing out about two minutes earlier and once everything quieted, the beasts began moaning, rolling in the sand, holding their heads.

Anna decided this was good…though seeing this pain, it carved deep into her chest. These poor creatures had lived on this island, peacefully most likely, for how long? Then came the Japanese military. And now here she was, she and the rest of the Chances Taken crew. She wondered if she'd know if any of the crew died the way these beasts understood their brethren were being harmed—for surely that was it, with all those rifle shots and all this pain.

But also, maybe this was her chance to escape. They were utterly sidetracked by anguish. Anna sprang to her feet, kicking dual waves of sand out behind her, and bolted toward the opening in the woven wall of the jungle fortress. Almost instantly, one of the sasquatches gave up on its wailing and reefed her back, sitting her painfully back on her throne.

"Okay. Okay," she said. "I'm sitting. Don't hurt me."

She picked up a handful of the berries they'd brought her and popped a few into her mouth. She'd nibbled before, found they tasted okay, a little sour, but didn't make her feel sick. Now she eyed the creatures. She'd have to play nice, pretend to accept all they had planned for her.

Two more beasts returned, offering a series of animated grunts and slaps, which seemed to make something clear to the others. Then it happened again, and all the beasts looked to the sky, as if sensing something terrible. The two that had just returned darted back through the opening in the nearly endless greenery.

The minutes began to mount and Anna wondered if this was life now. Was there any real hope? Were any of the members of the Chances Taken even alive? Had they departed the island to seek help? Jesus, they were days from anywhere, and most of their power was shot. How long would she have to wait for rescue? Was rescue ever coming? God, was this life now?

Through the greenery, two furry backs appeared. The fur was so coarse. Anna envisioned it rubbing against her—what really did they want with her? *Oh, God!* These sasquatches were shorter, hunched over. They moved clumsily, entering butts-first. Anna frowned as she weighed the oddity.

The others watched the two beasts curiously. The pair paused a moment and made a sound so low it was indecipherable, but sounded like English, like a word. They jumped then, spinning tightly, pointing rifles at the other sasquatches.

Anna blinked rapidly, her mind reeling. There was her father and there was Darvin, both wearing sasquatch pelts like Halloween costumes. They began letting off rounds from rifles covered in sand.

"Dad!" Anna shouted.

Two of the beasts quickly tumbled and it was

looking like victory. Anna burst from her throne once again and raced toward her father.

"Oh, fuck," Darvin said, trying to yank the bolt of his rifle. One of the old rounds had jammed somewhere in the barrel. He dropped the rifle and lifted the clawed hands of the pelt he wore, as if to give these sonofabitching things a taste of their own weaponry.

Maurice took down a third and aimed for a fourth when a beast tackled him, sending his rifle off into the sand and well out of reach. He rolled as he landed. The beast couldn't pin him right away.

"Stop!" Anna screamed.

Another of the sasquatches charged at Darvin and Anna saw it coming just in time to leap onto him, knowing—so she hoped, oh Christ, how she hoped—that they wouldn't attack him if it meant harming her. She was their goddess 2.0, of that she had no doubt. She'd had hours upon hours to think about it, to understand her plight.

The beast did indeed switch direction, skidding sideways into the sand before somersaulting back to its feet. The one on top of Maurice pinned him, holding him down like a mother on a sugar-buzzed toddler. The third remaining beast, shot and bloody, limped toward Darvin and Anna, murder in his face.

"Scratch me," Anna hissed over her shoulder.

"What?" Darvin said, boiling and reeking inside the sasquatch hide.

"Scratch me and threaten to kill me. Do it!" Anna said.

The beast got to two feet from them. Darvin raked claws along Anna's neck and shouted, "I'll kill her!"

The words surely meaningless, though the tone and action together spoke a universal language. The beast stopped, eyeing Darvin with angry, murderous eyes.

For close to a minute, all was quiet but for the huffing of breaths and a distant, but quickly approaching set of footfalls.

36

Vivian came to on the beach. The inhaler she'd sniffed from was now full of sand. She was alone and knew, damned well *knew,* she couldn't face whatever was happening sober. If any of what she had seen, even a little bit of it, was real, she had to get high. And what of before that stuff with the huge animal?

Had she confessed?

She thought yes she had and that was very bad business.

"Fuck," she said.

She pulled her cargo shorts onto her lap and began rooting through the bulky pockets. At least they'd left her stash when they stripped her.

Or did she strip herself?

And where the hell did all the cuts come from?

Both searching hands came upon prizes. She pulled out a wrapped syringe and her baggy of cocaine. For a tiny glimmering second, she noted the mess she'd become before a word shined upon her mind, brightly as neon in a starless night: SPEEDBALL.

When drugs weren't hitting quite right, it was time to up the ante. It's not like she could go with her earlier plan and quit, not now, maybe after she tried this one little thing.

She dumped a big bump of cocaine onto the paper package from the syringe. She withdrew a serving of morphine from the bottle with the syringe and shot it onto the cocaine bump. Everything mixed nicely and she dipped the tip before she pulled the plunger to suck up the goodness. She didn't need to tie off, she was thin and worked with her hands, which left her with plenty of good vein options popping from her sunburnt flesh.

The needle went in and the speedball filled her system. Almost instantly she was up and energized. Her head jerked back and forth like a chicken, sounds coming to her in a way that was downright freaky. This high was very good but also bad. Was she freaking out? Christ! She didn't care for the sounds suddenly around her at all and broke into a run. Quickly she was surrounded by green fronds. The sandy dirt of the forest floor was cool on her feet. But those damned sounds, they were still behind her, chasing her maybe. No, not maybe, absolutely chasing her.

"No. No," she said, huffing the repeated syllable after gasping a deep breath.

She tripped as she raced and fell face first into a pond. The water was horrible, the worst thing ever. The sounds got twice as loud as she hacked up the water that had invaded her system. She struggled to shore and kept on running, shooting down a well-trodden trail. Ahead, she saw a bear rug and knew she was about to be in her uncle's basement from childhood. He'd shot that bear himself, told her so while she was sitting on it, watching a VHS cassette of *Pinocchio*. That had been, oh, how long ago?

She got closer and the sounds behind her were like the void screaming back: pure terror. She closed her eyes and screamed herself, counterbalancing the weight of the noise behind her with noise in front of her. Nothing would stop her, she was running through the gate of the jungle kingdom, on her way to—she tripped over the corpse of a sasquatch. Her body flew, her arms swinging for purchase. Her toes pointed down like a ski-jumper. She seemed to go on forever and only stopped when her chin struck the empty altar throne next to the ancient bones, and she rolled into a fleshy ball.

The others and the remaining sasquatches watched in amazement. Unbeknownst to Vivian Montero, she'd produced a solution to a standoff.

37

Tim watched for the lifeboat charge back to the ship. He'd had time to slip away from his post to cover the bodies—including the sasquatch corpse they'd taken as proof of this misadventure—and grab a six-pack of Pabst and a bag of Mrs. Vickie's Jalapeño potato chips. He stood in wait, yawning regularly, desperate for rest, eating and drinking, hoping against logic that the costume gag would work, knowing it wouldn't.

But there they were, buzzing back to the Chances Taken, and with Anna. He hooted, punching the sky in celebration with his good arm, raining beer down upon his shoulder and head. The lifeboat got into place and Tim hit the button.

They rose quickly, though it seemed to take forever.

"How the hell'd you pull it off?" Tim said.

"Traded Vivian for Anna," Darvin said and grabbed a beer.

"We can't leave her there," Anna said and then snatched the chip bag.

"Bullshit," Maurice said. "Tim and Anna, you come to the bridge. Darvin, you mind the engine room. We're getting the hell out of here before they get a mind to exact some revenge for their fallen comrades."

2021 CE

The two hunter sasquatches who'd been trolling the actionless western shore of the island felt a different and almost as awful psychic ping as they had before. They departed their kingdom, feeling the pull of distance. Not just death, but distance. Someone had stolen one of their brethren. They raced through the forest, around the beach, and chased after the lifeboat.

Mixed in with the human interloper corpses was one of their own, they knew it, felt it so fully that they couldn't deny the need to rescue it. But they'd be smart. They watched the lifeboat rise up onto the huge ship. No good. They began swimming around the base, searching out opportunity. Dents and barnacles. They climbed and leapt until a rope gave them easy access up the side.

Once aboard, they grew wary and cautious. They sought the humans, watching them push through steel walls. They couldn't fight head on, not on this unfamiliar turf. They veered away and began testing walls for movement. One used claws at a crack and discovered a stairwell that led down into the darkness, and endless smells.

The beasts sidelined their mission for now to explore, only panicking once they heard the engines roar and felt movement beneath them. They hunkered down, waiting for the right time to act.

38

Vivian came to and found that she'd crashed hard. She sat up and looked around her. Three sasquatches watched her. She closed her eyes. "Tripping," she said and opened up after an internal twenty count.

The beasts were still there.

They converged upon her as a unit and the shock was so deep that she couldn't fight them, couldn't do much of anything but make like a board and plank. They lifted her. They set her on her seat at the altar. She eased some, physically. Mentally she was ready to jettison the coop for good, live somewhere in La La Land.

When she finally spoke, she meant to say, *What do you want?* But instead said, "Well, shit."

The End

Check out other great
Cryptid Novels!

Ian Faulkner
CRYPTID

Be careful what you look for. You might just find it.1996. A group of 14 students walked into the trackless virgin forests of Graham Island, British Columbia for a three-day hike. They were never seen again. 2019. An American TV crew retrace those students' steps to attempt to solve a 23-year-old mystery.A disparate collection of characters arrives on the island. But all is not as it seems. Two of them carry dark secrets. Terrible knowledge that will mean death for some – but a fighting chance of survival for others. In the hidden depths of the forests – man is on the menu. Some mysteries should remain unsolved...

Eric S. Brown
LOCH NESS HORROR

The Order of the Eternal Light, a secret organization have foretold the end of the human race. In order to save all humanity, agents of the Order must locate the Loch Ness Monster and obtain a sample of its blood for within in it is the key to stopping the apocalypse but finding the monster will be no easy task.

Check out other great

Cryptid Novels!

P.K. Hawkins

THE CRYPTID FILES

Fresh out of the academy with top marks, Agent Bradley Tennyson is expecting to have the pick of cases and investigations throughout the country. So he's shocked when instead he is assigned as the new partner to "The Crag," an agent well past his prime. He thinks the assignment is a punishment. It's anything but.Agent George Crag has been doing this job for far longer than most, and he knows what skeletons his bosses have in the closet and where the bodies are buried. He has pretty much free reign to pick his cases, and he knows exactly which one he wants to use to break in his new young partner: the disappearance and murder of a couple of college kids in a remote mountain town.Tennyson doesn't realize it, but Crag is about to introduce him to a world he never believed existed: The Cryptid Files, a world of strange monsters roaming in the night. Because these murders have been going on for a long time, and evidence is mounting that the murderer may just in fact be the legendary Bigfoot.

Gerry Griffiths

DOWN FROM
BEAST MOUNTAIN

A beast with a grudge has come down from the mountain to terrorize the townsfolk of Porterville. The once sleepy town is suddenly wide awake. Sheriff Abel McGuire and game warden Grant Tanner frantically investigate one brutal slaying after another as they follow the blood trail they hope will eventually lead to the monstrous killer. But they better hurry and stop the carnage before the census taker has to come out and change the population sign on the edge of town to ZERO.

Check out other great

Cryptid Novels!

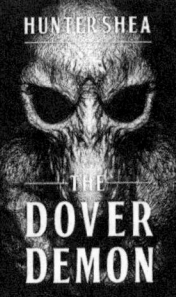

Hunter Shea

THE DOVER DEMON

The Dover Demon is real...and it has returned. In 1977, Sam Brogna and his friends came upon a terrifying, alien creature on a deserted country road. What they witnessed was so bizarre, so chilling, they swore their silence. But their lives were changed forever. Decades later, the town of Dover has been hit by a massive blizzard. Sam's son, Nicky, is drawn to search for the infamous cryptid, only to disappear into the bowels of a secret underground lair. The Dover Demon is far deadlier than anyone could have believed. And there are many of them. Can Sam and his reunited friends rescue Nicky and battle a race of creatures so powerful, so sinister, that history itself has been shaped by their secretive presence? "THE DOVER DEMON is Shea's most delightful and Insidiously terrifying monster yet." – Shotgun Logic Reviews "An excellent horror novel and a strong standout in the UFO and cryptid subgenres." –Hellnotes "Non-stop action awaits those brave enough to dive into the small town of Dover, and if you're lucky, you won't see the Demon himself!" – The Scary Reviews PRAISE FOR SWAMP MONSTER MASSACRE "B-horror movie fans rejoice, Hunter Shea is here to bring you the ultimate tale of terror!" – Horror Novel Reviews "A nonstop thrill ride! I couldn't put this book down." – Cedar Hollow Horror Reviews

Armand Rosamilia

THE BEAST

The end of summer, 1986. With only a few days left until the new school year, twins Jeremy and Jack Schaffer are on very different paths. Jeremy is the geek, playing Dungeons & Dragons with friends Kathleen and Randy, while Jack is the jock, getting into trouble with his buddies. And then everything changes when neighbor Mister Higgins is killed by a wild animal in his yard. Was it a bear? There's something big lurking in the woods behind their New Jersey home. Will the police be able to solve the murder before more Middletown residents are ripped apart?